Praise for Byrd

"Addie is a particular woman—a character that will linger and grow beloved—but she could also be your sister, your roommate from college, a friend in the neighborhood. She's still struggling in her thirties to make sense of old loves and loss that keeps cycling back into her life. A successful woman in the world, her heart remains in flux until love that can't be budged finally takes root in her. Kim Church has imagined a world of good people missing the mark, as good people sometimes do. They're familiar, a comfort. I will never forget the impact of the final pages."

—Patricia Henley, National Book Award finalist and author of *Other Heartbreaks*

"This protagonist is so appealing, with her unflinching moral candor, her mistakes based on generous instincts. The prose is lilting, joyous. This novel—about young lives that start out full of promise, falter, then recover—is a hard-luck story that will make you feel good."

—Debra Monroe, author of *On the Outskirts of Normal: Forging a Family Against the Grain*

"Fresh, riveting, and brilliantly written. The richly layered story explores motherhood and its attendant relationships in ways that break new ground, both stylistically and thematically. Already recognized for her work in the short story form, Kim Church should gain national attention with this original and important novel."

—Angela Davis-Gardner, author of *Butterfly's Child* and *Plum Wine*

"Beautiful, dream-like language...connects us directly with the experience of the characters. It goes right to the heart, without being filtered through the brain, the way a smell connects you to a memory."

—**Nancy Peacock,** *New York Times* **Notable author of** *Life Without Water* **and** *The Life & Times of Persimmon Wilson*

"Kim Church has created an unforgettable and gripping tale about a young woman's passage to adulthood in a small town in North Carolina in her excellent debut novel, *Byrd*. There are books we like to read because they provide a window to a world wholly unfamiliar, but there are others like *Byrd* that give insight into our own lives: our hopes and dreams, what we've done right, opportunities missed."

—*BookPage*

Byrd

Byrd

Kim Church

DZANC BOOKS

DZANC
BOOKS

5220 Dexter Ann Arbor Rd.
Ann Arbor, MI 48103
www.dzancbooks.org

BYRD

Book design by Steven Seighman
Cover art by Ilsa Brink

Published 2014 by Dzanc Books

ISBN: 978-1938604522
Second edition: March 2014

This project is supported in part by awards from the National Endowment for the Arts and Michigan Council for Arts and Cultural Affairs.

Printed in the United States of America

10   9   8   7   6   5   4   3   2

The world is never ready
for the birth of a child.

—Wislawa Szymborska, "A Tale Begun"

for my mother
in memory of my father
and for Anthony, always

Byrd

Dear Byrd,

This is how I told your father.

We climbed up on his roof. We could see the ocean, wrinkles of light in the distance. I was wearing a billowy cotton skirt. I wanted to look soft, unthreatening, unselfconsciously pretty. I wanted your father to love me. My legs were pale, not used to sun in winter. I had painted my toenails lavender. I wanted him to be a little sorry he hadn't loved me all along.

The roof of his apartment was flat, asphalt. All grit and sparkle.

He was glad to see me, he said. He didn't ask why I'd come back.

He unfolded an orange blanket from his sofa bed and we laid out our picnic: smoothies, crinkle-cut fries from his favorite stand on the beach, canned peaches from his kitchen, and barbe-cue I'd brought from home, packed on dry ice. So much food. I had to make myself eat. I chewed slowly, counting each bite, the way you're supposed to, though I couldn't remember how high to count.

A warm breeze ruffled my skirt.

Your father offered to spike my smoothie, but I covered my cup with my hand.

I wish I could tell you we were young, inexperienced, not yet grownups or ready to be. That's the story you're expecting, isn't it?

We were thirty-two. We'd grown up together. Everything about the afternoon—our picnic, the roof, the sun, the salty air, your father's pilled orange blanket, him sitting close and warm beside me—had been coming all our lives.

After we'd eaten, when I couldn't put it off any longer, I told him my news, the news I had carried across the country to deliver in person. I thought if I could see him when I told him, I would know what to do.

I was delicate, telling him. Artful, as I'd practiced. So artful he didn't understand at first what I was saying. He blinked like the sun was hurting his eyes. The big white California sun, dazzling, warm even in February.

I.

Unborn

Swimming

Carswell, North Carolina, August 1965. The summer before fourth grade, the summer before Roland. Addie is playing with her little brother in the blow-up pool under the poplar tree, in the shade. Fair-skinned children. Claree, their mother, doesn't want them to burn. She is hanging laundry.

"Stop!" Addie yells.

Sam won't stop splashing her. He is five, small for his age because of asthma. He splashes her again, his hand flinging a few drops of water in her face, her eyes. One in her mouth at exactly the wrong instant. It catches in her throat—so small, a tiny droplet. Who could choke on a tiny droplet? But Addie's throat closes, and when she tries to breathe, nothing happens. She pulls for air, she pushes. Nothing. Her head starts to feel tight like a tied-off balloon. Her face gets hot. Her eyes water.

"What's the matter?" Sam says, taunting, little-brothery.

Addie jumps out of the pool and runs to her mother. Sam runs after her.

"What, honey?" Claree says.

"I didn't do it," Sam says, crossing his arms over his chest. He is shivering, his swim trunks dripping.

Addie moves her lips. *Help*, she tries to say, *I can't breathe*. But her mother doesn't understand, or doesn't know what to do. Seconds are going by with no air, and Addie doesn't know which neighbors are home or if she could get to them in time or if they could save her anyway.

Finally her mother clicks into gear. She grabs Addie from behind and presses her bony fists under Addie's ribs—once, twice, three times, until the air comes. Not the big gulps Addie wants, but a thin, whistling stream. Enough, but just barely.

Sam starts to cry. His crying turns to wheezing.

Claree puts her arms around both of them and kneels down. Addie expects her to tell them everything's fine, not to worry. But she just keeps kneeling until she is all the way on the ground, sitting in a patch of moss with her dress billowed out around her, the blue laundry dress with big pockets for clothespins.

Roland's last Alabama summer. His family is about to move to North Carolina, where he will start fourth grade in a classroom where the desks are set out in a circle instead of rows, and the teacher, Miss Overcash, wears tight seersucker dresses that show the raised outline of her bra. When she calls roll he will answer "present" instead of "here" and everyone will laugh, kids with crew cuts and pigtails and teeth too big for their faces, all staring because he's the new boy and his shirt is paisley instead of checks or stripes. His favorite shirt, worn just to impress them. A girl with green eyes and long thin red braids will stare hardest. She won't even pretend not to. Addie Lockwood. She will stare so hard he will have to look away.

But not yet. Not today. Today he's still in Birmingham and Dooley is his best friend and they're at the swimming pool like any other day of any other summer. Except today, as a parting gift, Dooley is teaching him how to dive.

They start on the edge of the pool. Dooley shows him how to bend his knees, lift his arms, cross his hands. He shows him how to tuck his chin to his chest. The idea is to go in clean, without a splash.

Roland has good form. He does everything Dooley says. What he doesn't know, what Dooley hasn't told him because Dooley doesn't know either, is that you can tuck your head too tight, you can curl all the way under yourself in the water and come around and hit your head on the side of the pool.

All he will remember is plunging in, the thrill of going under headfirst, water rushing up and closing around him, swallowing him, the music of it. A burbly, muted symphony.

When he wakes up he is lying on the pavement with people standing over him. Everything, everyone glistens, Dooley most of all, with his slick white hair and blinking, bloodshot eyes.

"Not bad for your first try," Dooley says. "You almost nailed it."

Dear Byrd,

What's your name now, I wonder. Not Blake, I hope, or Blair. Or Smitty. Please, not Smitty.

I can guess what you're thinking: what mother would name her child Byrd?

But I knew the name wouldn't follow you. Which is partly why I chose it—I wanted a name no one else would ever call you. One thing about you that would be only mine.

What I first loved about your father was his name. It was lyrical, something you might hear in a song or read in a book.

Not that anyone would ever write a book about him. Or that he would ever read it.

Queen of Mind Beauty

Addie believes in books. They are more interesting than real life and easier to understand. Sometimes you can guess the ending. Things usually work out, and if they don't, you can always tell yourself it was only a book.

Also, there's the paper-and-glue smell of them, and the way the pages turn soft from being read and re-read.

In first grade, Addie's teacher gives reading prizes: for every twenty-five books, a silver dollar, or, if you prefer, she'll drive over to your house after supper and let you choose a toy out of the trunk of her car. Addie always invites her over. She likes having the teacher's giant black Chevrolet parked out front where the neighbors can see. She likes standing over the trunk, inspecting the dolls, cradles, jump ropes, Slinkies, kickballs, knowing any of them could be hers. In the end, she is always practical. She collects enough silver dollars to fill a peanut butter jar, which she keeps on her dresser. It makes her feel rich and important, like someone you might read about in a book.

————

In fourth grade she sits next to Shelia DeLapp and watches her practice her cursive: the slow, fat letters; the way Shelia bites her tongue when she writes; the way her hands sweat and make the notebook paper bubble up. At the end of every word, Shelia lifts her pencil off the page and rolls it around in her fingers to redistribute her weight on the lead.

Shelia spells her name with the *L* before the *I,* prettier than the way most people spell it, even though she pronounces it the same. *She-la.*

She is plain and shy, with a round face and slippery black hair that falls out of her barrette. Her eyes wobble when she's nervous, a condition she was born with.

She invites Addie to her house after school, the green house behind the car wash. There's a hole in the front porch; you have to be careful walking in. They sit at the kitchen table and play Crazy Eights. There's a breeze; the curtain bats the window screen; the car wash whirs. Shelia's hands sweat and make the cards sticky.

"I saw you staring at the new boy," she says to Addie.

"I wasn't staring."

"He doesn't even *look* at you when he looks at you."

"I heard he hit his head at the swimming pool. I heard it did something to him."

"Hitting your head doesn't make you stuck-up."

The new boy's long legs jut into the aisle. His hair is shiny and dark as Coca-Cola. Addie once gave a boy her ice cream dime to let her touch his hair. It was short and flat on top—a brush cut, which she imagined would be stiff like the bristles of a toothbrush, but it was soft, like her father's softest shoe brush.

The new boy writes left-handed, and when Miss Overcash calls him to the board for his times tables, he stands close, his elbow over his head and his face almost against the board so that no one can see his wrong answers until he's finished. He gets chalk dust on his shirt from standing so close. Miss Over-cash has to brush him off. It's embarrassing to watch, but thrill-ing, too, like watching someone get punished. He stands very still and stares out the window as if he's somewhere else, as if that isn't chalk dust flying off *his* shirt.

In the cafeteria he bites his ice cream sandwich into a differ-ent animal shape every day. People call out: *Giraffe! Elephant! Bear!* Addie calls out, but he never makes hers. Once he was making a rabbit so she said *Rabbit!* But then he changed it into something else.

She thinks his name sounds like a place. Roland Rhodes. A faraway place. One that would take a long time to get to, and once you did, you would never want to come back.

"The Rhodes woman came in today," Addie's mother an-nounces over supper, which is canned ham, canned green beans, and sliced cranberry sauce. "The new doctor's wife. Act-ing like a doctor's wife."

Addie's father makes a face. "He's a chiropractor."

Her mother laughs the way she does when something isn't funny. A small, sour sound.

Her parents do this every night, complain about people they know, or used to know, or barely know, or don't know at all.

"Roland's in my class," Addie says.

"First time she'd set foot in the store and she wanted to take five dresses out on approval. Said her daughter didn't have pa-tience for shopping. I wanted to say, What child does?"

Addie's mother works at the Carousel Shoppe selling expen-sive girls' dresses to mothers who don't have to work. Dress-up dresses: Peaches 'N Cream and Polly Flinders and Ruth of

Carolina Originals with sashes and built-in crinolines and Peter Pan collars, stripes and plaids all perfectly matched at the seams. She can buy dresses for Addie because of her employee discount—the only part of her job she likes. As soon as Addie outgrows girls' sizes she plans to quit and get an office job.

"Roland has nice clothes," Addie says. She closes her eyes and remembers his paisley shirt, the swirls of blue and purple and green.

"Your clothes are as nice as anyone's," her mother says, and reaches over to cut up her little brother's ham.

After dinner their father leaves the table and their mother tells stories. "Tell the one about the birthday cake," they say, and Claree tells about the time when she was a girl and baked a cake for her father, their grandfather. A sheet cake with lavender frosting. She hid it under her bed, planning to surprise him. That evening while she was cooking supper, her mother went upstairs and found the cake, slid it out from under the bed, stomped on it and smashed it flat. Then walked down to greet Claree's father, her shoes thick with frosting.

"Those big black orthopedic shoes," Claree says. "She always had trouble with her feet."

Addie and Sam laugh. They think the story is supposed to be funny.

Sam is four years younger than Addie, with eyes gray as nickels and hair so short you can't tell what color it is.

Addie has red hair, which she is not allowed to cut. Girls aren't supposed to cut their hair. Her mother's hair comes all the way to her knees, black with a long silver stripe, her birthmark. No one at Addie's school has a mother with hair as long as Claree's.

Addie's father works at Reliable Loan Company, in a building on West Fifth Avenue that used to be a house. The company has a billboard on the highway, a giant picture of a dollar bill, but instead of George Washington, there's Bryce Lockwood in his big square glasses and plaid sport coat. When the sign was new he would take the family for rides in the car just to look at it.

At school, Addie is the Dollar Man's daughter.

Bryce's gold velour armchair and ottoman take up the middle of the living room. He likes to stretch his legs while he watches TV. Their set has rabbit ears and thirteen channels on the knob. When it's time for a different show, Bryce makes Sam change channels.

"While you're up," he tells Sam, "how about grab me another beer?"

Sam goes in the kitchen, brings back a cold can of Schlitz, hands it to his father.

"Come a little closer," Bryce says. "I want to tell you something."

"Don't," Addie says. "It's a trick."

But Sam doesn't listen. He never listens. He leans over, hoping to be let in on a secret, a joke, something Addie wouldn't get, and Bryce flicks him on the head with his middle finger, the way you thump a melon. Sam's head makes a sharp, hollow sound.

Their mother sits at one end of the sofa, leaning against the arm, her long black hair splayed out across the plaid upholstery. It looks clingy, like cobwebs. She watches TV as hard as she can.

In middle school everyone has to take P.E. The girls wear starchy blue gym suits with snaps down the front. Sally Greer, the first in their class to develop, is always popping out of hers. Sally tells everyone she's dating Roland Rhodes. "We made out under the bleachers," she says.

After school, Shelia's mother, Betsy, makes them glasses of Tang, the drink of the astronauts, with Tang ice cubes. Betsy knows how to make everything better. She works the early nursing shift at the hospital and gets off before school is out; by the time Shelia and Addie get home, she's changed out of her white uniform and into her afternoon clothes: baggy shirt, pants, unlaced brogans—old clothes her husband, Shelia's father, left behind. He's been gone for years. Shelia doesn't remember him.

"Staying for dinner, Addie?" Betsy ties on her apron, reaches under the cabinet, and lifts out a white coffee-can-sized can with no label, just MEAT in big black letters, which she plunks on the counter. "Could be pork chops."

"Sure," Addie says, "I like pork chops."

Betsy has short hair, which she cuts herself and dyes yellow. She is loud like a man, and likes to whistle.

Addie rolls a Tang ice cube over her tongue and lets it plunk into her glass. "What's 'make out'?" she asks Shelia.

Shelia frowns; her eyes wobble.

"It means," Betsy says, and slings a spoonful of Crisco into her frying pan, "you get by on what you've got."

Bryce gets paid on Fridays and takes the family out to dinner. Afterwards, he stops in the VFW for a drink. Addie and Sam wait with Claree in the car. Addie slides down low in the back seat in case anyone walks by.

"I would never do this to my children," she says. She is thirteen.

"You don't have children," Sam says.

Claree, facing the windshield, says what she always says. "He won't be long."

"This is yours to keep." The health teacher solemnly hands each girl a pink booklet. "Take it home and read it."

The other girls roll their eyes. They've already started. They don't need pink booklets. Shelia has started. Addie is the only one who hasn't. She rolls her eyes along with them, but secretly she can't wait to get home and read her booklet.

It has line drawings. The writing is clear and direct. "During your cycle," it says, "you may feel bad about your body. Pamper yourself. Take a scented bubble bath. The water should be warm but not hot."

She memorizes her favorite parts. "Warm but not hot."

High school.

Girls huddle in the hall talking in whispers, pretending not to notice when people eavesdrop. They wear makeup. They wear halter tops and hip-hugger jeans that show their navels. They carry little purses for their lipstick and lunch money and cigarettes. Boys love and fear them. Addie sometimes wishes she were one of them. She wishes she were one of anything.

She reads. She reads *Catch-22* by Joseph Heller, and *Franny and Zooey* by J.D. Salinger. She believes Franny and Zooey have something to teach her, even if they're high-strung and always talking in italics, even if the things they call phony, things that *really get under their skin*, are things that only privileged people or New Yorkers ever have to deal with. She recites Franny's Jesus prayer. She goes on Franny's cheeseburger diet. She doesn't have a mystical experience, but the ritual is comforting. Eaten every day, even a cheeseburger (she likes hers with pickles and mayonnaise) can be holy.

She reads *The Teachings of Don Juan: A Yaqui Way of Knowledge. One Flew Over the Cuckoo's Nest. A Separate Peace. Huckleberry Finn. The Heart Is a Lonely Hunter. To Kill a Mockingbird. A Clockwork Orange. Light in August. Brave New World. Mrs. Dalloway. In Cold Blood. The Stranger. All the King's Men.* She reads *Daybreak* by Joan Baez and *Tarantula* by Bob Dylan, a book that makes her decide to write poetry because she sees how you can write anything and call it a poem.

She and Roland have one class together, an elective called "The American Counterculture" taught by Mr. Saraceno, a young teacher with horn-rimmed glasses and black hair that curls down onto his shoulders. He wears jeans and blazers with patched elbows and comes from "places too many to name."

They read the Beats: Kerouac, Ginsberg, William Burroughs. They talk about sex and drugs. They can't believe they have a teacher like Mr. Saraceno in Carswell, and figure he'll get fired when their parents find out what he's teaching.

In his class, Addie is outspoken, brazen, always raising her hand, always arguing. "Why weren't there any women Beats? It's not like women hadn't already been part of the literary scene. Look at Edna Millay in the twenties. She wrote better than any of these guys. She was a bohemian. She was sleeping with everybody in Greenwich Village while Jack Kerouac was being fussed over by his mother and all those Catholic nuns who thought he was some kind of saint."

"There were women Beats," Mr. Saraceno says.

"Spectators," Addie says. "Disciples. They sat around listening to all that crap poetry, snapping their pretty fingers. They cooked and cleaned and had sex and helped their men get famous. And ended up in mental hospitals, hanging themselves. They didn't write, and if they did, why aren't we reading it? They were nothing like women now. Look at Joni Mitchell. She's a poet *and* a painter *and* a musician." She pauses to catch her breath. "You know, Mr. Saraceno, American counterculture didn't begin and end with the Beats."

Roland, sitting in the desk behind hers, leans forward. "Tell it, baby," he whispers. She can feel his breath in her hair.

Smokers congregate at the wall outside the Language Arts building after class and light up. The guys walk out in a row, three or four across, bent-kneed, jeans scraping the ground, long hair fanning out over the collars of their denim jackets. They lean against the wall and shake cigarettes out of Winston and Camel and Marlboro packs, cup their hands around matches, narrow their eyes, lean back, blow smoke rings, flick ashes.

Addie sits on the ground, the brick wall warm against her back, her composition book open on her knees, her long red hair falling around her like a curtain.

Betsy in her wrinkled shirt
makes coffee out of kitchen dirt.

She tries to write like Edna, like Joni, with rhythm and rhyme.

I'm seventeen, my skin is pale,
my eyes are green, I bite my nails.
I wish that I were someone else.

When she writes, the rest of the world disappears. She doesn't notice when Roland sits down beside her.

"Can I see?" he says.

This is the first time he's ever sought her out. He barely knows her, though she knows everything about him. He's a musician, a guitarist. He has a Fender Stratocaster strung backward so he can play it left-handed. His favorite thing to talk about is music; his favorite music is the blues. Duane Allman is his hero. He is still mourning Duane's death.

When he talks about music, people flock to him. When he talks, he's a star.

He doesn't wear his hair long. He doesn't wear T-shirts or jeans to school. His mother, Pet, won't allow it. Pet is famous for her rules. Roland has to wear corduroy pants, shirts with collars.

He doesn't complain or apologize when he talks about Pet; he talks about her like she's a character in a book. His Pet stories make him popular. Because of her, people are kind to him. Girls especially.

"I mean, if it's okay," he says to Addie. "I don't mean to be presumptive."

"Presumptuous," she says, and hands him her notebook.

A red-haired woman sings the blues
to skinny boys in lace-up shoes.
She sings because they ask her to.
She sings and they applaud her.

She sings "My Baby" by request—
they always like the slow ones best.
You'd think by now they would have guessed
she's Janis Joplin's daughter.

He reads slowly, moving his lips. His bangs fall in his eyes. He pushes them away and they fall again. He pushes them away and looks up. "Have you ever tried putting your words to music?"

"No. I'm just trying to write poems."

"This is good," he says. "This is good enough for a song. I play guitar, you know. I've got lots of ideas for tunes but no lyrics. Maybe we could write something together."

"Maybe," she says. They've never had a real conversation and here he is, asking her the most personal thing imaginable. *Write something together.*

"What are you doing this afternoon?" he says. "I'll be practicing, if you want to come over."

This is how Roland's mother greets her: "Is Roland expecting you?" Pet has a sharp face and beauty-parlor hair—frosted, with tight curls. She doesn't offer Addie a drink—no Tang or iced tea or lemonade or tap water—even though it's a warm afternoon and Addie has walked a long way.

The Rhodes house is in Country Club Hills, a brick house with green trim—not grimy-schoolroom green like Shelia's, but a clean, pale, yellow-green Roland's mother calls celery. Everything inside, too, is celery—walls, carpets, countertops, vinyl floors.

"Roland's in the basement," Pet says, and leads Addie to the stairs.

What Pet calls the basement is actually a giant sun-filled room with sliding glass doors that open onto a patio. There's a wet bar and a fireplace and a TV and a console stereo and all the furniture you can think of, plus Roland's guitar and amplifier, and still so much empty space you could turn a cartwheel across the floor.

"You came," Roland says. "I didn't know if you would."

He puts on the Allman Brothers, *At Fillmore East*, and plugs in his guitar. This is how he practices, playing along on "Whipping Post" using Pet's brown glass Valium bottle as a slide. He sits on a bar stool, bent over, his dark bangs hiding his eyes, as if he has to go to some secret place to find the song. He plays fast, putting in lots of extra notes, filling every space with sound.

Addie slips off her shoes, draws up her knees, and basks in the moment—sun slanting in, the plush celery armchair, Roland playing for her. A moment as unlikely as it is perfect.

It's a long moment. "Whipping Post" is a twenty-two-minute jam, all of side four. When the song ends, the tone-arm on the stereo retracts, and Addie applauds. "You're amazing," she tells him. She feels like a Beat woman, except Roland really *is* amazing, worthy of applause.

He sets his guitar in its stand. "Too much, wasn't it? I got a little carried away. I'm not used to an audience. I need a cigarette."

She follows him out onto the patio, into the yard, to a shady spot behind a tall row of boxwoods. He lights a Camel, takes a drag and passes it to her.

"Who do you listen to?" he says, casually exhaling a plume of purple smoke, as if the question were casual, which Addie knows it is not.

She wants to say the right thing. She could humor him and say Dylan or the Stones or Howlin' Wolf. None of those would be a lie. She could be ingratiating and obvious and say the All-mans. "Joni Mitchell," she says.

"Right," he says, "of course," and laughs.

"She's a genius."

"She's got that fluttery voice. It gets on my nerves."

They finish their cigarette and go back inside and Roland starts the song again from the top. This time he relaxes into it, holding notes, bending them. He turns up the distortion on his amp to get a bluesier sound, more like Duane. That raw, run-down, lied-to sound.

Addie closes her eyes. The less he tries to impress her, the better he plays.

He's almost at the end—it's all double-stops and chords now, loud, wailing, building to the full-on heartbreak of the final chorus—when they hear a pounding overhead.

Pet.

"Roland," she calls from the top of the stairs, "you have homework."

He stops abruptly, without protest, without complaint, as if he'd been expecting the interruption. He turns off his amp, takes off his guitar, wipes the neck with a chamois cloth, then lays it gently in its case, the way you'd put a child to bed. He turns off the stereo, lifts his album by its edges and slides it into its cover.

"I like listening to you," Addie says.

"I like playing for you," he says. "You and me, we're not like everybody else."

That night she lies awake in her blue bedroom with her headphones on, listening to Joni, whose high, sad voice drowns out everything. She tries to imagine *being* Joni—brilliant, beautiful, always in and out of love, able to write and sing and paint about it. Joni even has her own music company, Siquomb, a word she made up, an acronym for "She Is Queen Undisputedly of Mind Beauty." Addie tries to imagine herself as queen undisputedly of anything.

Flower Street is quiet. Every now and then a car drives by, flashing its headlights through the dotted swiss curtains. Addie imagines it's Roland coming for her in his father's Buick. She imagines him parking along the curb, lighting a cigarette, waiting. There's no time to get dressed. She will slip out in her nightgown, run barefoot across the grass. Her feet will get wet from dew. She won't be able to see his face in the dark, only the glowing orange tip of his cigarette. He'll push open the passenger door and say to her, *Come on, let's drive to the lake.* And they will, they'll drive to Old City Lake and park near the dam, and the night will be spacious and peaceful with only the lapping of the water, and she'll lean against him and point at the trees on the far bank and say, *Look, lightning bugs.*

"I love how you're not afraid to speak up," Roland says. They're at the wall, sharing a smoke between classes. "I love all the shit you know. How do you know so much?"

"I read," she says.

"I don't. The only book I've ever read start to finish is *On the Road.*"

"Too bad you didn't pick a better one," she says.

His laugh is like a dry cough. *Huck-huck-huck.* Self-conscious, like he's laughing at the sound of himself laughing. "I had a head injury when I was young. My brain hurts when I read."

He tells her the swimming pool story. He tells it as if he's letting her in on a secret he's never told anyone, and she pretends she's hearing it for the first time.

"Music is how my brain works," he says. "Ever since I hit my head, the only way I can think is in music. Which is cool when you're playing guitar, but not when you're not."

"Most people would kill to play like you."

"I just wish I knew how to do anything else," he says.

She reaches over and touches his hand. If she were a Beat woman, this is when she might kiss him. Not a real kiss, no big deal. Lips lightly brushing lips. A suggestion of a kiss.

"I love how he lets me hear his mistakes," Addie tells Shelia. This is the first time they've played cards since she started spending afternoons at Roland's.

Shelia plays the ten of spades. "You're such a groupie."

"Girls, hush," Betsy says. She is frying fruit pies and watching the Watergate hearings on the little TV she has moved into the kitchen. Watergate is Betsy's soap opera. She knows all the characters. Her heroes are Senator Sam from North Carolina, with the gavel and the eyebrows and the deep drawl, and Howard Baker from Tennessee. Two Southern gentlemen politely bringing down the government.

"I don't get it," Shelia whispers. "It's not like he's Eric Clapton."

"He's good," Addie says, "but that's not the point."

On TV, Senator Sam bangs his gavel. Betsy turns off the frying pan. The kitchen smells like apples and brown sugar and grease. "Shelia," she says, "take a dollar out of my purse and you and Addie take my car to the Winn-Dixie and pick up a carton of ice cream to go with our turnovers. Vanilla or butter pecan, you girls decide."

A Saturday like every Saturday. Bryce is up early for his golf game, which means the whole house is awake. Addie pads into the kitchen, where Claree is serving Bryce's breakfast: scrambled eggs, soft, with a dash of Tabasco. She sets his plate on the table, and his coffee. She watches him butter his toast like it's his dying act. Addie knows what she's thinking: this is the last time today they will see him sober.

Sam comes in and pours himself a bowl of Lucky Charms, carries it to the living room, sits down on the floor in front of the TV and turns on Road Runner cartoons. He's wearing his idea of a golf outfit: knit shirt, khaki shorts with long pockets for collecting golf balls, Hush Puppies, and white socks with red rings around the top. He has worn a spot on the carpet from camping by the front door. He studies the TV screen, his face bright, hopeful, his whole body tense, as if maybe Wile E. Coyote's latest Acme device will be the one that finally works; maybe this time he'll trap the Road Runner. Sam is so intent, he seems not to notice when Bryce comes through the room. Bryce has to step over him on his way out. "So long, buddy."

Sam doesn't answer. On TV, Wile E. Coyote gets blown up. Again.

Outside, Bryce's car pulls away. Sam finishes his cereal, takes his bowl back to the kitchen and rinses it, then heads outside to play kickball with the kids across the street. Their noise fills the house—high-pitched voices yelling made-up rules, the rubbery thumping of the ball.

Half an hour later Sam is back, red-faced and wheezing, his golf clothes dirty.

"Are you okay?" Addie asks.

He drops into Bryce's chair and puffs on his Primatene inhaler until he has enough breath to talk. "He never takes me golfing."

"Why do you even want to go?"

Addie pictures Bryce and his friends on the golf course, humming around in their little carts. Sun pounding, dew boiling off the grass, the hot green smell of everything. After every hole they tip their flasks and wipe their mouths on the backs of their hands. Bryce tells a joke and they all laugh. He tells the punch line again and they all laugh again. Bryce laughs hardest.

He's glad to be away from home, glad not to know about Sam getting red dirt on his chair, or Claree in the back yard in her pedal pushers, hair piled on her head, sweat streaming down her face, trying to start the mower, or Addie, who's about to desert them both and escape out the front door, just like he did.

Pet and Roland's sister have gone shopping in Greensboro, his father is out buying gas for the lawnmower, and Roland's been getting high, Addie can tell. His eyes are bloodshot and he smells smoky-sweet.

She follows him downstairs. He opens the stereo, puts on an album and sits down beside her on the sofa. The sofa is fat and soft. Roland is wearing his Saturday clothes: white T-shirt, cutoff jeans, and crew socks with spent elastic. He props his feet on the coffee table. His socks bunch around his ankles.

There's a crackle from the stereo, then a swell of strings.

"What's this?" Addie asks.

"A surprise."

The music is lush, an orchestra, nothing like what they usually listen to. Roland sits closer. His leg touches hers.

"Want to dance?" he says.

They get up and he puts his arms on her waist. The music rises and falls. They stand close, swaying gently, barely moving.

"What *is* this?" she asks again. Not that it matters. He's holding her. Music to be held by.

"Percy Faith. 'Theme from A Summer Place,' the old man's favorite. Romantic, isn't it?"

She rests her head on his shoulder. No more talk now. Only the swelling orchestra. Only the dance.

Until, from above, a roar—a car in the carport. A single slam of a car door.

Roland doesn't lose the rhythm. He keeps swaying, not letting go.

More sounds from the carport. Clanks, thunks, sputtering, and a small explosion—Roland's father starting the mower.

Roland stops. "I've got an idea," he says.

She always imagined sex would be mysterious. That it would happen in a dark, quiet place. Not in Roland's parents' room on a bright Saturday with the sun squeezing in through closed blinds and a towel on the bedspread to keep it clean. Not with Roland's father's lawnmower making loud circles around the house, growling past the bedroom window.

She thought Roland would say things. Kiss her.

She thought it would take a long time. She didn't know it was possible for him to finish so soon: the minute he touched her, before he was even inside her.

She thought that afterwards she would be the shy one, that he would be the one to hold her and ask if she was okay.

She thought he would tell her not to leave, not yet, instead of rolling off the bed and scooping up his clothes and ducking into the bathroom and turning on the faucet and calling out over the water that it's too bad she can't stay.

"Sex changes everything," Shelia says.

"It wasn't really sex," Addie says. "We stopped before it got that far."

"Good thing," Shelia says.

They are in Betsy's pushbutton Dodge, driving to the health clinic, a flat brick building on the highway. They pull into the gravel lot and park in back so that no one can see the car from the road.

Before they can get their pills they have to sit through a class with girls they don't know while a nurse explains their bodies. The nurse puts diagrams on an overhead projector. She passes around a big doll to show them how to check their breasts for lumps. When it's Addie's turn the other girls break out laughing. "Them doll baby titties bigger than hers," one says.

"Class," the nurse says.

If sex changes everything, not-sex changes everything even more.

This is what Addie learns in high school. If you're a guy, if you're Roland, it might be okay to fail French or algebra, but it's not okay to fail at sex.

And if you're a girl, if you're Addie, there's nothing you can do or say to make it okay. She would like to tell Roland, *Please, it doesn't matter.* But it does matter, all of it—the dance, him watching her undress, their bodies touching while his father's lawnmower rattled outside, his bare, slender ass when he rolled away from her. What happened between them was as intimate and daring as she imagines sex could ever be.

They don't talk about it. Every day, they sit together in counterculture class, they share cigarettes at the smoking wall, and they don't talk about it.

She doesn't want to go back to his basement without an invitation and he doesn't invite her, so they don't talk about it there.

Weeks go by and they don't talk about it.

She asks about his music.

He's putting together a band, he says, a blues trio. They practice in the drummer's garage. "We're going to play for senior assembly."

"That's great," she says.

He doesn't invite her to the drummer's garage.

He doesn't ask to read her new poems.

They don't write a song together.

A Friday night in late May. The air is warm and humid, full of the smell of cut grass and burning charcoal, almost too thick to breathe. A thunderstorm would be a relief, but no one wants rain for the party, which is a cookout because Pet doesn't want Roland's friends coming in the house.

There are two long tables pushed together in the carport with "Happy Birthday" tablecloths and plates and napkins and streamers and balloons. Addie sits at the far table, across from Danny Brewster with his stringy ponytail and too-tight "Keep On Truckin'" T-shirt. He keeps glancing out at his car parked along the curb. Danny's car is his life; it's all he talks about. A shiny banana-yellow Barracuda with a black 440 decal, fender fins, chrome wheels, wide tires. He sat in it for his senior picture.

Roland is at the head of the main table, flanked by his sister and her friend Louise White. Louise is a sophomore whose older brother died in Vietnam. People at school treat her like a hero.

Addie doesn't believe in war.

Louise has strawberry-blond hair and freckles. Whenever Roland talks, she laughs, tinkly as a bell. Roland passes her things out of order, the hot dogs and chili before the buns, the baked beans twice before anyone else has had them. Even Pet is kind to her, sprinkling her with questions like how is her father getting along and what's she going to do this summer. Louise sits up straight and holds her elbows at her side and delicately pinches her fork. Her dad, she says, has lined up a job for her at the tile plant, second shift. She's grateful he could get her on, jobs being so scarce and all. She's trying to save money for college.

She is so open, so uncomplaining.

Pet tut-tuts and says she's sure Louise will get a scholarship.

Louise smiles serenely. She has a heart-shaped smile and straight white teeth. "I hope so," she says.

She lives behind the Presbyterian Church, in a yellow house with an ivy-covered yard. When her brother died, her mother had a breakdown. Now Louise has to take care of things at home and isn't available for after-school activities. But she's popular anyway, because of her perfect smile and perfect figure, and because she knows how to act in any situation. Tonight she's smiling, sugary, but when she and Roland's sister pass Addie in the hall at school, they look down and don't speak.

"I love this neighborhood," she says. "My grandfather remembers before they built the golf course or any of these houses, when this was all farmland. He and his friends would come over in winter when it snowed. They would start up there"—she points, her arm sleek and confident—"and go sledding all the way down to the creek. It's one long hill, if you look at it."

Roland's parents are fascinated—the idea of people sledding through their living room! Roland stares at Louise like she invented snow.

"Remember those big round Coca-Cola signs?" she says. "They could get three people in one of those signs. But there was no way to steer, so they'd go spinning like crazy and about half the time end up in the creek."

"I know where we can get one," Danny Brewster says loudly, to nobody.

"Where I grew up," Pet says, "it never snowed. That's one thing I've liked about moving up here, how it gets cold enough to snow."

"It used to snow more," Addie says. "Even in my lifetime. I remember when I was small, it snowed more than it does now."

"I wouldn't want any more," Pet says.

Roland's birthday cake is from Fancy Pastry, chocolate, in the shape of a cutaway electric guitar. Everyone sings the birthday song, Roland makes a wish and blows out his candles, and Pet cuts little pieces of cake that everyone eats with plastic forks, scraping the frosting off their plates. Before they can ask for seconds, Roland stands up.

"I want to thank you all for coming." He speaks in his deep, practiced, performer's voice. "You're the best friends anybody could ever have."

"Keep on truckin'!" Danny yells.

"I wish you could stay here forever. I really do. And"— laughing his dry, amused-with-himself laugh—"you can if you want to. But I've got to go. I promised Louise a ride, and she has to be home by nine thirty."

No one else laughs. Louise blushes, but only slightly, as if she can control even the flow of her blood. Addie glares at Roland but he ignores her. Of course, she thinks. He doesn't want to know how he's wrecked her night. She's here without a car or a ride home; she walked over hoping he would take her home, hoping that, for at least the short drive down Fairview, they could be alone again. Now he's leaving without her, leaving his own party, and it's too late to call her parents. Claree can't drive at night and Bryce will be drinking. He would come anyway if she called, driving fast and loud like he does, screeching up to the curb, blowing his horn.

Roland doesn't want to know any of that.

He opens the car door for Louise, closes it behind her, gets in and drives away. Addie imagines them cruising across town, Louise telling stories, Roland *huck-huck*ing, laying his arm along the seat behind her. Louise leaning her head back.

He won't just drop her off. He will walk her to her front door. Addie pictures them standing there, Roland pressing his hand into the small of Louise's back, waiting for her to invite him in.

Louise's house will be quiet and clean: no blaring TVs, no spilling-over ashtrays. Louise's father will be sitting up in the den, reading a magazine under soft yellow lamplight, listening to jazz on the radio. Louise will whisper to Roland, "He's so protective." Which will make Roland think about Louise's dead brother and broken mother and feel sorry for her. He will kiss her—not on the mouth; on the cheek, maybe, or forehead. He will take his time with her. He'll think to himself, *With this one I'm going to get it right.*

Across the table, Danny Brewster taps his plastic fork on his plate. Danny has a horse-shaped face and thick glasses that make his eyes seem closer than they are. "I can give you a ride," he says to Addie, more quietly than she knew he could talk.

"Can we leave now?"

"Fuckin' A." Danny forks up his last few crumbs of cake and pushes himself up from the table. "Far-out party," he tells Roland's parents.

Addie doesn't bother with goodbyes or thank-yous.

The yellow 'Cuda gleams under the streetlight. "Hop in," Danny says, opening the door. The seat is slippery, like it's been polished. Danny cranks the engine and his eight-track blasts Edgar Winter, the bass boosted so loud it rocks the car. Addie buckles her seat belt. She hopes Roland's parents are watching. She hopes they all are. She hopes the neighbors are flocking to their windows.

Danny reaches into the glove box and pulls out a joint big as a cigar. "Happy birthday, Roll," he says, and hands Addie a lighter. "Do the honors?"

"Fuckin' A," she says.

———

Late that night, when her family is sleeping, Addie sneaks out of bed, tiptoes into the kitchen, lifts the receiver on the new harvest gold wall phone, and dials Louise White's number.

"Hello?" Louise says, her voice muffled. "Hello, who is this?"

Addie hangs up.

She calls again the next night, and the next. One night Louise's father answers. Addie starts hanging up faster, before anyone can pick up. She starts calling at all hours. Midnight, five in the morning, different times—whenever she's near a phone. During the day, when no one's home, she can let it ring longer. She can let it ring and ring and ring.

Addie's senior yearbook contains no evidence of Roland-and-Louise, even though at school they have become one word. There are no pictures of Roland propped against Louise's locker, none of him with his arm draped across Louise's shoulders or smiling at Louise from the stage during senior assembly. All the pictures are from before.

There is no evidence of Roland-and-Louise in Roland's inscription to Addie. He fills her entire back page, as if she'd been saving it for him.

> *Addie,*
> *You made life very interesting for me this year. I am really appreciative to you for all the things you gave me. You have a way of reassuring me like nobody else can.*
> *I hope we can see each other this summer. I'm sure we'll see each other at the beach after graduation. That's really going to be wild. After that I doubt I will be around too*

much because the band and myself are going to lead very
secluded and mysterious lives living together somewhere.

When I think back on high school I think, what a
waste of our formidable years. I really am glad to be mov-
ing on, although the future for me is unpredictable. All
I can say when someone asks me what I'm going to do is
"other plans." No one would understand if I told them my
real ambitions. You are one I think that can understand to
some degree what I am trying to pull off.

Lots of love and luck,
Roland Rhodes

Underneath he has drawn a genie lamp, a flat thing with
a curved spout and a cloud coming out. His words are in the
cloud, as if by magic—Addie's wish, being granted.

Beach

But they don't see each other. Graduation week at Ocean Drive is supposed to be for graduates, but Roland brings Louise and rents a motel room instead of sharing one of the big houses with everybody else. Addie imagines them sunning by the motel pool, Roland rubbing Louise's back with coconut oil while he tells her the story of his diving injury.

They don't show up at any of the parties. This ought to be a relief, but Addie is in no mood to feel relieved.

At the last party on the last night, she gets drunk and loses her virginity once and for all, to J.C. Green. They don't plan it; she and J.C. barely know each other. They just happen to be the last ones still conscious after everyone else has gone home or to bed or found another place to pass out. They are sitting on a gritty sofa in the living room of a big oceanfront house. Someone has left the tone arm of the stereo cocked back and a Doobie Brothers album plays endlessly. Addie doesn't know why she came to the party at all or why she's still here. She gets up to leave and staggers, whirly-drunk. J.C. catches her. He's fat, with a beery, greasy smell, mildly sickening. But his fatness is also a comfort, something to sink into.

Addie lets him hold her. She can feel a thumping through his jeans, like a lowdown heartbeat. She doesn't care. She lets him turn her around and fold her over the arm of the sofa. She lets him take down her striped shorts and hump her from behind to the beat of "Long Train Runnin'." J.C. is relentless and annoying, like the song, which she will never be able to listen to again.

She thinks of Roland. This is his fault. Because of him, nothing is special.

She Leaves

All year, Sam watches his sister leave.

He watches her leave for school every morning—the same time as him, but not the same school.

He watches her graduate, orange sash across her gown.

After graduation she leaves for the beach. A week later she comes home sunburned and won't talk to anyone.

That summer she leaves every morning for her job at the library. She goes out after work every night, he doesn't know where. Weeks go by when he doesn't see her at all.

At the end of summer she leaves for college.

"Write me letters," she tells him.

He does. In the beginning he writes to her almost every week.

Dear Addie, we got a new TV with a remote control. Now Bryce can change his own channels.

Dear Addie, they won't let me try out for sports.

———————

Dear Addie, I took my bicycle apart, cleaned and lubricated all the parts and put it back together. It flies.

Dear Addie, Bryce fell. In the kitchen. He hit his head on the counter. We picked him up and Claree put a cold washcloth on his head.

Dear Addie, thanks for the sweatshirt. What exactly is a Spartan?

Dear Addie, the Davenports came over for a cookout and Bryce set the poplar tree on fire.

Dear Addie, they have a new rule at school. Everybody has to be in a club. I was in the chess club but there were only two of us and it got boring. I joined the travel club but we never traveled, we just sat around looking at slides. So my friends and I started our own club, the Apathy Club. For Homecoming we made a banner, MAY THE BEST TEAM WIN. It won for Most Appropriate, but no one went to pick up the prize.

Dear Addie, this time he fell in the street and Mr. Davenport had to help us bring him in.

Dear Addie, when are you coming home?

Dear Addie, I can't wait to be the one who leaves.

Greensboro

The university is forty minutes and a world away from Carswell.

A world of books—at the heart of campus is a gleaming new library tower, big as God.

A world of flyers—on every wall in every building, on every telephone pole on every street corner, flyers advertise readings and concerts and lectures and rallies and auditions and art openings and roommates wanted and things for sale, cheap.

A world of rolling lawns and majestic shade trees and people reading, arguing, laughing, making out, working calculus problems, playing guitar, playing Frisbee, playing Hacky Sack. There's always someone to talk to, someone to go to the new film festival at the Janus with, wander the bars of Tate Street with, smoke pot and eat Mexican food with. Addie is infatuated with all of them. Jimmy the physics major, who cooks her pancakes in his dorm room. Stephen, who does yoga and smells faintly of patchouli. Geoff with a G, who shows her his poetry, which is so raw and wild and charged she decides to give up trying.

No one gives her the deep-down panic of real love, the jolt she always felt with Roland. But Roland would not fit in this place. She thinks of him only rarely, and with only the smallest tug of sadness—for him or for herself, she couldn't say.

She studies literature—the seventeenth-century metaphysical poets, the Germans in translation. She studies history and Latin and logic, which she loves for its perfect reliability. She studies the philosophy of literature, the philosophy of science. All of her philosophy classes are taught by the same professor—a compact, muscular man with round glasses, neatly combed hair, and neatly pressed shirts tucked into neatly pressed pants. He never lectures without a piece of chalk in his hand and never strays too far from the board.

He lectures about retrocausality. He draws pictures of the space-time continuum on the board to show how the future influences the past, except he doesn't use those words.

"Is it the same as predestination?" the class asks.

The fallacy of that question, he says, lies in the use of "pre-". There is no before or after, no pre- or post-. No past, present, or future. "Every event," he says, "affects every other event."

He is intense. When he talks, a bead of white spittle forms in the corner of his mouth. He has hair in unexpected places, on his knuckles and elbows and the undersides of his forearms. He tells Addie she's the best student he's had.

She has never felt so important.

Roland, on the road with his band, wonders if he will ever feel important again. He tries to think of himself as an adventurer like Kerouac, fearless and crazy and free. It would help if he could write like Kerouac, though he doubts even Kerouac could find poetry in this cramped, stinking van. Or in guys who are always fucking each other's women, using up each other's drugs, fighting over money, which there is never enough of, and never bathing or brushing their fucking teeth.

All he ever writes is an occasional postcard home. He likes the plain black ones that say "Georgia at night," or "Louisiana at night." Keep his parents guessing. Sometimes he calls them. Always collect, always from a different place—a payphone or somebody's apartment.

He doesn't think about Carswell. Louise with her allover freckles, or Addie with her long hair. Her green eyes watching him like he was somebody to be watched.

She goes home only when she has to. Once for Shelia's wedding to Danny Brewster. Shelia and Danny both stayed in Carswell; Shelia became a certified medical assistant and Danny is working as a mechanic at the Plymouth dealership until he can open his own garage. They hold their wedding reception at the brand-new clubhouse of their brand-new apartment complex. Music blares from a boom box—Danny's wedding-music mix tape. "I hope you brought your suit," Shelia says to Addie, to everyone, as if she expects them to swim. No one does. People dance barefoot by the pool—hospital people, car people, people Addie doesn't know. Who would have thought you could find a whole new set of friends in Carswell?

Danny asks Addie to dance and she says yes even though she has a cheap-champagne headache that the song, "Brown Eyed Girl," is only making worse. But she came to celebrate, and she is genuinely happy for her old friends, even a little envious. "Congratulations," she yells at Danny over the music. "You and Shelia have it all figured out. I can't even decide on a major."

Nobody tells you what the road can do—the greasy fast food, the speed-laced drugs. Every club is another piss hole painted black, every club owner a crook. The same women line up after every show.

His mother thinks he's out making a name for himself. "You're seeing it all," she says when he calls home.

"I sure hope not," he says. Because what he's seeing is all the same. It's not some great romantic adventure, not like Kerouac. The deal with Kerouac was, he could come in off the road any time he felt like it. And he always had somebody, his mother or his old lady or some friend's old lady, waiting to feed him chicken soup and wash his socks while he sat in some nice room writing his masterpiece.

Addie works at the Readery, a secondhand bookstore in a decrepitly elegant Victorian house on Mendenhall Street. She lives in an apartment on the top floor, with tall ceilings and faded wallpaper and heart pine floors and braided rugs and, outside the front window, a magnolia tree with big clean-smelling blossoms. Her landlord-slash-boss is a lumberjack-looking man named John Dunn, like the poet but with a different spelling. "Batter my heart!" Addie likes to call to him from the stairs.

The Readery is open only at night. It's the hub of Greensboro's intellectual nightlife, where professors convene to read, drink coffee, smoke, listen to scratchy records, and say things to provoke and impress each other. Addie's philosophy professor sometimes stops in. He doesn't sit around pontificating and arguing with the others. He's a loner, a browser, always coming up to Addie with some question. Has she noticed that both these books were dedicated to the same person? How can she be sure the author's signature is authentic? Would she mind putting on this album (always jazz) instead of whatever is playing?

He stays late. Some nights after closing she goes upstairs to her dark apartment and looks out her window and there he is on the sidewalk below, his face upturned, street light shining on his glasses.

Roland moves with the band to Texas, to an apartment with roaches the size of his feet.

The professor is the last customer in the store. Addie asks if he'd like to see her apartment. He follows her upstairs.

She puts on Joni Mitchell, *For the Roses*. They sit on the sofa and she peels a tangerine and offers him slices.

"Sweet," he says. Tangerine juice dribbles down his chin. He is like a character in one of Joni's songs.

Dear Byrd,

I have learned that it's possible to become satisfied with your life too soon.

Flames

The professor and his wife celebrate their anniversary as usual, by going out to dinner. They sit at their regular table near the bar, their hands folded in front of them, their rings giving off a dull glow. There is a white linen cloth on the table, a small oil lamp, and a red flower in a glass vase. The professor trusts his wife to know the name of the flower, and to remember it, so that days from now, if he's looking for a way to make conversation, he can ask her, "What kind of flower was that in the restaurant, the red one?" And she'll answer him, and for that instant they can remember tonight and it will be as if they're back at this starched white table, listening to piano music.

They begin with cocktails: Campari and soda for him, vodka martini for her. They don't have to order; the waitress remembers. The professor is flattered to have his drink remembered, even though no one else drinks Campari. As usual, he will leave an extravagant tip.

His wife cocks her head while the waitress recites the dinner specials. The waitress doesn't bother with menus; they never order from the menu. It's an unspoken rule with them. Whereas when the professor takes Addie to a restaurant (never this one, where he'd be recognized) she insists on reading everything in sight. She is a glutton for words.

"I'll try the salmon," his wife says.

"I'll have the same," he says.

She is a small, shapely woman, his wife, with a blameless face and a small, disapproving mouth. She's wearing her navy blue out-to-dinner dress with a pearl choker.

The professor sips his drink. It tastes bright and bitter and gives him a sweet, heady feeling. Not drunk, but on the verge.

Addie strides into the restaurant in her boots, feeling powerful. She feels like making a scene. Then she sees them at their table in their dress-up clothes, their faces tired, glazed over. And she knows at once there will be no showy ending. There's nothing left to end.

It ended, she can't say when, not with a big drama but with a lot of little ones. The night the professor sat on her sofa looking miserable and she asked him what was wrong and he said, he actually *said*, "Sex with my wife isn't so good lately." And the time he showed up late for their day-after-Christmas dinner wearing a shiny new leather jacket, peanut-butter brown, with a zipper and an elastic waistband that made the belly balloon. A gift from his wife. Addie wanted to poke it, deflate him. She could have forgiven him for being late, but not for that jacket—for having the nerve to wear it, for having a wife who would pick out something so ugly.

Lately everything has felt like an ending. The sandpaper scrape of his loafers on the stairs, his light tapping on her door. The way he still pretends not to presume, even though he keeps clothes in her closet and a toothbrush and razor in her bathroom. Even though her once-airy apartment has taken on the dark, garlicky smell of him.

It feels like an ending every time she sees him standing there, smiling and false.

The professor tries to ignore Addie. She's at the bar, next to the piano player, who's on his break. She takes a cigarette out of her purse, taps it on the bar—a habit the professor has always found annoying; he can almost hear it over the din in the restaurant—and the piano player offers her a light. He uses a real lighter, not a disposable. He talks, and Addie nods and makes a show of listening.

The professor isn't fooled. He knows why she's here.

He thinks back to his first night in her apartment. "I have a policy," she said, "against getting involved with my professors." A policy she honored for as long as she was a student, which was years longer than most people.

From the beginning, he was clear about what he could offer and what he couldn't. He and Addie made a point of not letting whatever they did together get in the way of what they did apart. He knew she saw other people. Sometimes she was unavailable for months. But even that on-and-offness, that in-betweenness, was something. There was energy in it, possibility. It made his marriage tolerable.

He doesn't know when she first started having different expectations, when her vocabulary changed, when she first started using words to hurt him. When he stopped being brave, adventurous, risk-taking, and became a coward.

He *is* a coward. If he didn't know it before, he knows it now, tonight, on his anniversary, in his favorite restaurant, the only place in Greensboro that serves Campari, while Addie sits at the bar flirting with the piano player.

She cups her hands around her wineglass and rests her mouth on the rim, not quite drinking. The professor is the one who taught her about wine, and about jazz. He introduced her to Merlot and Coltrane, Shiraz and Thelonious Monk.

The flame in the oil lamp is sputtering. The professor polishes off his drink, sets down his glass, and right away the waitress brings their dinner—salmon topped with white caper sauce, rosemary-roasted sweet potatoes, and his favorite, grilled asparagus. He bites into a spear. Smoky, delicate, still slightly crunchy. Delectable.

Addie can see them reflected in the mirror over the bar, picking at their food, not talking to each other. She isn't jealous. Guilty, a little. Mostly she's angry—with herself for having wasted so much time, with him for being such a cliché. How did she not see that right away? A married, middle-aged college professor with hairy knuckles. Too smart to be wise, too horny to be good in bed.

She should leave the restaurant now. But the piano player is talking to her. He has long brown hair, a gray suit, a nice smile.

"Beautiful blouse," he's saying. "It matches your eyes. The same dangerous shade of green."

It's not the obvious flirting that intrigues her. It's that word, *dangerous.*

She holds up her wineglass and pretends to examine it. "I can't remember all the esses," she says.

"Sorry?"

"The way you're supposed to drink wine. There are five esses. 'See,' 'swirl,' 'sniff,' 'sip,' and something else, I can't remember."

"'Swallow'?"

"No."

"'Spit'?"

"No." Addie laughs.

"I've got it," the piano player says. "'Stay.' You sip your wine and stay through my next set and I'll buy you dinner." Without waiting for an answer, as if he's already sure of her, he leaves her at the bar and returns to the piano.

She can see his hands on the keys—long, sleek, manicured, confident hands. You'd have to be a musician if you had hands like that. Or a surgeon. He's playing "Spain" by Chick Corea. Every note is perfect, polished. Every note gleams.

He looks down when he plays, concealing his face. The way Roland used to play guitar.

Roland's music was different—rougher, full of mistakes. But the blues is *about* mistakes. Mistakes and suffering. To play the blues, Roland once said, you have to reach down into the saddest part of yourself. "That's where the music is," he said.

She hasn't thought about Roland in a long time. The memory of him comforts her somehow, makes her warm. She can feel heat rising, blooming in her face.

While his wife nibbles at her chocolate torte, the professor watches Addie and the piano player eat off each other's plates and carry on animated conversation, their voices rising as if they want to be overheard. Addie drops names. "Bill Evans…" "…like Keith Jarrett." "…with Gary Burton." Musicians she would never have heard of except for the professor.

The fact that he has no right to be angry only makes him angrier.

As if sensing his attention, Addie gets up. She is wearing a shiny emerald green blouse over tight black jeans. She starts toward the ladies' room, then makes an elaborate detour, doubling back to his table. His wife looks up. Her cheek is flecked with chocolate. The professor has never felt sorrier for her, or loved her more, or been more ashamed of himself for wanting Addie. And he does; he wants her more than ever.

"Sorry to interrupt," she says, and lays her hand on his arm. Her hand is warm, her face flushed. "I just wanted to say good-bye." She leans toward him, her hair swishing forward, brushing the table.

Instinctively, he closes his eyes. He is terrified, thrilled, swallowed up in the moment. *In every present moment, the past and future converge.* When he opens his eyes, Addie is gone, so suddenly he wonders if he imagined her.

His wife sets down her dessert fork, sighing, as if the fork has become too heavy, a burden she can no longer bear.

"Full?" the professor says.

Dear Byrd,

Even now I don't know why I thought to call your father after so many years. It's a question I've often asked myself. Here are some possibilities.

1.   I was feeling stupid and small and wanted someone to make me feel special like your father once did. You and me, we're not like everybody else. *Maybe he said that to everyone, I don't know, but when he said it to me, it seemed true.*

2.   I wasn't thinking of the times he had not *made me feel special.*

3.   I'd heard from a friend that he was working as a musician in a famous place I'd never been. He had followed his dream, chased it clear across the country. He'd been brave in a way I hadn't, and I wanted to congratulate him.

4.   I had lived too long among academics.

5.   Astrologically I was due for an adventure—north node in Sagittarius.

6.   Retrocausality. This is how my philosophy professor would have explained it. At a point farther down the space-time continuum was a child waiting to be brought into the world. I called your father because you wanted to be born.

California

"Hello?"

"Roland?"

"Donna?"

"No. Addie. Addie Lockwood, remember?"

It's early December 1988, a Sunday afternoon. Outside her window the magnolia tree glistens with ice. There is a chilly quiet in the apartment, throughout the house; the store is closed—one reason she chose today to make her call. She has been up since early morning. She practiced in the shower what she would say. *I met a man who looks like you. He has your hands.* She's wearing her blue sweater. She's wearing makeup. She wants to feel pretty, even if he can't see her. For the last hour she has been sitting on her sofa, wrapped in her softest quilt, telephone on the coffee table in front of her, a scrap of paper with his number, and a bottle of Beaujolais, now half-empty. The wine makes her brave; it also makes her sad for having to spend so much bravery on a single phone call.

"Addie? I can't believe it. I was just thinking about you."

"No you weren't." *Who's Donna?* she wants to say.

"Okay, not really, but damn, baby, it's good to hear your voice. Are you okay, is everything okay?"

"Everything's fine. I was—there was this guy, this piano player—"

"You just break up with somebody?"

She twists the phone cord around her finger. "As a matter of fact, yeah," she says.

"I knew it. A breakup call. It's okay. Tell me all about him."

"Oh no, that would put us both to sleep. Anyway, this isn't a breakup call. I just wanted to talk to you. I heard you were in L.A. making music and it made me happy and jealous. You're doing what you always meant to do."

"Venice Beach, actually. Yeah, it's totally wild out here. It's fucking paradise is what it is. I'm four blocks from the beach. You can see the ocean from my roof."

His voice is so familiar she can feel it, humming through her like electrical current. "Wow," she says.

"Who told you where to find me?"

"Danny Brewster. Well, Shelia, but Danny told her. He works on your mother's car."

"Danny that used to sell loose joints?"

"He married my friend Shelia and opened a garage."

"You're in Carswell? I thought you left."

"Greensboro. I came here for college and stayed."

She pulls her quilt tighter. She can hear the tick of freezing rain outside her window. On the phone, too, in the background, there's a faint tapping. Then silence. Roland sniffs. Another pause. He lets out his breath.

"You still writing poems?" he says.

"Not since high school. I read like crazy, though. I work in a bookstore."

"That's so *you*. I always loved that about you."

"What?"

"Everything. I'm just flattered as hell to hear from you."

She pours another glass of wine. "Tell me about you," she says. "What are you up to?"

"Same thing as everybody else out here. Show business. I work for a company that builds movie sets. Ready Set. Get it?" He laughs his old laugh, *huck-huck-huck*.

"What about music?"

"Yeah, you know, I'm playing out some, making some contacts, trying to pick up some session work. I was on the road for fucking ever. I came out here and I said, never again. This is the place, man. This is where shit happens. Have you been?"

"To California? No."

"You ought to check it out. It's wild."

"I hear the weather's perfect."

"You'd love it. You should come, you really should." He's getting loud, insistent. "Come see me. Come for Christmas."

"What?"

"Or New Year's. Come spend New Year's with me. I'll show you a good time."

She waits for his laugh. He used to do that—let people take him seriously, then laugh. Even when he was serious he thought it was funny when people took him seriously.

"We'll have a blast," he says. "It'll be just like old times, only better."

She can't believe she's having this conversation. She still can't believe she picked up the phone and dialed Roland's number and he answered.

She knows better than to take him seriously. Even if L.A. at New Year's is exactly the kind of adventure she needs.

"My astrologer says I should travel," she says.

"Always listen to your astrologer."

"Is this a serious invitation, Roland?"

"Abso-fucking-lutely."

She packs early. She hopes that packing will make the trip seem real. She packs her paisley skirt, her tightest jeans, her black boots, her black jacket. She is thrilled and sickly nervous; she's also (though she wouldn't admit it) embarrassed to be traveling back in time to someone she used to know. Is this the only adventure she could come up with? Hasn't she outgrown Roland?

And what must Roland think? Does she seem as lonely and desperate and pathetic to him as the professor now seems to her?

"I'm going to California to spend New Year's with an old friend," she tells John Dunn when she asks for time off. She says it casually. *California.* A word luscious as a piece of fruit.

John Dunn doesn't ask questions, or point out that this trip isn't the sort of thing Addie does. "I'll give you a ride to the airport," he says.

She's braced for the obvious—the long flight, the strange city. But the flight is just a droning bus ride in the air. Los Angeles, too, is easy: a big, lazy, sprawled-out sunbather of a city where you can never be entirely lost because every street and neighborhood, every building, no matter how ordinary, is a place you've heard of.

She's less prepared for smaller things. The smell of diesel in the LAX terminal, making her afraid to breathe. The crush of people headed there, there, there. People with other people waiting for them. She claims her bag and finds a place to sit. She checks her watch, freshens her makeup, tugs at her dress and tries to convince herself she looks like someone a man would want to drive to the airport and pick up. Twice she calls Roland's apartment but there's no answer and no machine. She waits forty-five minutes. The crowd thins. She starts to panic. People actually stop for her. "Is there some problem, miss?" "Can I call someone for you? A cab?"

God deliver me, she thinks, *from the kindness of strangers.*

Then she sees him. She knows him first by his walk, lean and smooth, his feet gliding along as if they don't quite touch the ground. He's wearing a denim jacket and a black T-shirt that says "Déjà Voodoo." He has a mustache and his hair is cut in a mullet, short in front, layered on the sides, long in back. He looks like he just walked off an album cover.

"Baby," he says, "I'm sorry. I couldn't find a place to park." He smiles the lopsided, apologetic smile she remembers, and opens his arms, and she, too relieved to be angry, falls in.

She can tell from his apartment that there's a woman. Air freshener plugged into an electrical socket. An open box of baking soda in the refrigerator. A blouse in the closet.

There's only one closet; the apartment is an efficiency, no bigger than a motel room, with painted cinderblock walls and a filmy picture window. Roland takes her suitcase to the closet and pushes his clothes to one side, and there, crumpled on the floor in back, is a faded pink blouse with brown underarm stains. She pretends not to notice, but it gives her a quick, sharp pain, that blouse.

Roland invites his friends Pete and Golita over to meet her. "Un-fucking-believable," he tells them. "We haven't seen each other in, like, ten thousand years, and then out of the blue she calls me up, and now here she is."

"Nice." Pete nods. He has wild orange hair like the singer in Simply Red. He's sitting at Roland's counter tapping a small pile of white powder onto a mirror, chopping it with a razor blade, carving it into thin lines. He passes Addie a rolled-up dollar bill. "Company first."

"I don't know how."

"Breathe in. Don't breathe out."

She holds the dollar straw to one nostril, closes the other with her finger, and leans down. The powder burns her nose. Her eyes water. The back of her throat tastes bitter. Her ears start to buzz.

Roland touches her. "Okay?"

"Yeah, I'm good." She smiles at his feathered hair. She smiles at his apartment, so tiny, so—*efficient*. The sofa unfolds into a bed; the dinette table holds his phone, stereo, and portable TV; the floor lamp doubles—triples—as a table and magazine rack.

"So, Addie," says Golita. She has blue saucer eyes and a Carly Simon mouth. She is bosomy like Carly, dark blond, a singer herself. She sings nights and works days at Ready Set with Pete and Roland. "How come Roll never told us about you?"

On the boardwalk, which is not boards but pavement, everything moves fast and smooth and so do they, graceful as wild animals. Addie can't tell if she's walking or running or gliding or flying or dreaming. They serpentine through a strange circus of weightlifters, street skaters, men swallowing fire, guitar players on unicycles, women telling fortunes.

"The bar's around the corner," Golita says.

They follow her out of the crowd and into a small yellow building. Inside it's all dark wood paneling with a Maple Leaf flag over the bar, a jukebox on the far wall, and a single pool table in the middle of the room. Pete buys beer, Golita puts quarters in the jukebox and Roland puts quarters in the table. He hands Addie a cue stick and shows her how to hold it, standing behind her with his arms on hers.

"I'm a slow learner," she says.

"I've got all night," he says.

She loses every game. She doesn't care. "Buy me another round," she says. "Rack 'em."

They monopolize the table until closing time. They walk home a different way, past giant murals and cafés (they haven't eaten but no one mentions food; no one is hungry), under swishing palm fronds. The night sky has faded to purple—an incandescent, glowy purple. Out here, it never gets completely dark.

When Roland opens the sofa bed there is a smell like salted cashews. The smell of sex.

He offers to sleep on the floor but she tells him no, she doesn't mind sharing. She turns out the lights and gets in bed without taking off her dress. She rolls onto her side, facing the wall, her back to Roland, and listens to the muffled sounds of traffic from the street and the distant moan and hiss of the ocean. She listens to Roland, unzipping his pants.

He lies down behind her, slides his hand under her dress.

She touches his hand, guides it.

He doesn't hurry. He takes a long time this time. She doesn't think he'll ever finish.

In the morning, they shower together and towel off in the tiny bathroom. Roland opens a canister of mousse, sprays a little in his hand, lets it swell to the size of a golf ball, and works it into his wet hair. He hangs his head upside down between his legs and aims the blow dryer straight up—"for volume," he says, a trick he learned in show business.

"I want to know all your secrets," she says.

———

She falls in love with the sound of the ocean, a constant *whoosh* behind all the other sounds.

She falls in love with the sun, which is different here, expansive and white, bleaching everything, making even the ugliest buildings gleam like laundry on a line.

She falls in love with the unreality of the place. On Hollywood Boulevard they have to stop for a man in chaps crossing the street with his bull. On the Santa Monica pier, a man at the bar offers to buy her a drink.

"I'm Kin," he says.

"No, you're not," she says. "I know you. You're Scotty from General Hospital."

She falls in love with Roland's friends. One night they all go to dinner in a French café Pete knows, Maison Gerard ("the House of Jerry," Roland translates), with red walls and posters advertising French soap and cigarettes, and a French lounge singer, Serge Gainsbourg, on the sound system. Their waiter is an actor studying to play a French waiter. His face is flat and round as an omelet pan. While they wait for their meal, Pete spreads potted cheese onto rounds of French bread and deals the bread like cards. "So," he says to Addie, "wasn't the Lost Colony in North Carolina?"

"That's right. The first English settlement in America. By the time the new governor got there, the whole colony was gone."

Roland says, "Remember how in school they used to tell us, 'And no one ever knew what became of the settlers'? It was never any fucking mystery to me." He tomahawk-chops the table with his hand.

"That's just what they wanted you to think," Pete says. "Always blame the Indians."

"What's that Opie Taylor movie," Golita says, "where all the old people get in a boat and go to another planet and live forever?"

"*That's* what happened," Pete says. "They're probably on Mars right now, kicking up red dust."

"With silver buckles on their shoes," Addie says.

"Wearing top hats," Pete says. "Trying to grow maize, but it won't grow. 'We put fish in the ground the way the Indians showed us and still it *won't grow.*'"

Driving is her favorite drug. She becomes addicted to the motion, the forever-changing view. She loves watching Roland drive, how he stretches out his arm and drapes his hand over the steering wheel, every part of him long and loose. Whenever they come to a 7-Eleven he stops for pink wine and lottery tickets.

Late one night they drive up the coast to Zuma Beach with the windows rolled down. Salt air eddies in around them. Nina Simone purrs on the tape deck, "Since I Fell for You." Strings of Christmas lights glitter on wooden fences along the road. Beyond is the big dark ocean.

"You're shaking," Roland says. He pulls over and takes off his jacket, wraps it around her.

"Dance with me," she says, turning up the volume.

They get out and he pulls her close and they slow dance to Nina Simone right there on the edge of Pacific Coast Highway, a twinkling fence and an ocean on one side of them and the threat of traffic on the other.

When the song is over, they get back in the van and drive some more.

"I'm sure he's a sweet piece of ass," Golita says to Addie. "He's also a total fuckup. You know that, right?" The two of them are in Golita's kitchen. Pete and Roland are in the living room with the new Michael Jackson album turned up. "I mean, I love the man, and Pete's fucking *in* love with him. But he's a mess."

"How?"

"Oh, you know. He's always late. When it's his turn to drive we always get docked at work. He's the only person I know that ever runs out of gas. He's always running out of something. Money, coke. He loses stuff. Burns stuff. See my floor? I mean the landlord's floor that me and Pete will have to pay for." She points out a patch of brown blisters at the foot of the stove. "One night we left him alone to make popcorn and he plugged in the popper and set it on the stove and turned the stove on high."

"When he was young," Addie says, "he hit his head."

"In the swimming pool," Golita says. "Everybody's heard that story."

Pete knows a drummer in a bar band and arranges for Roland to sit in so that Addie can see him play before she leaves town. It's a nicer-than-average Venice bar, with tables and chairs and a tile dance floor. The band opens its first set with love songs: "Cold Love," "Part Time Love," "Hoodoo Love," "I Stole Some Love." Roland sits at the back of the stage, cradling his unplugged guitar, tapping his foot, fingering silent chords.

"Why isn't he playing?" Addie says.

"This isn't his gig," Golita says.

"He will," Pete says.

The band plays "I Feel a Sin Comin' On." Roland is stranded in the shadows.

"So what's going on with you and Roll?" Pete asks Addie. "You like him?"

"Sure. We're old friends." Addie takes a swig of beer, sets down her mug. "When's somebody going to tell me about the woman?"

Pete and Golita look at each other.

"I've seen her things in Roland's apartment."

"Elle," Golita says.

"Don't worry about Elle," Pete says. "She's just some chick who followed Roll home one night. You know Roll. What's he gonna do."

"He needed help with rent," Golita says.

"Where is she now?"

"Gone," Pete says. "Moved out. Don't worry. It's a good thing. Tell her, babe. You ever seen Roll this good?"

Golita shrugs.

"Look," Pete says and touches Addie's arm, "you want to step outside? Get some air?"

She gets up with him. They leave Golita to save the table.

The sand parking lot behind the bar backs onto a canal. Moonlight shivers on the water. "Like the real Venice," Addie says, though she has never been to Italy. There's a mattress on the bank, and a tire, and a broken shopping cart. Pete takes a brown bottle out of his pocket, unscrews the cap, which is also a tiny spoon, and offers it to Addie. He opens his jacket to shelter her as she lifts the spoon to each nostril.

"My doll's tea set had spoons like this," she says.

"You have a tea set?"

"My doll did. When I was young. I don't know what happened to it."

Behind the dull thudding of the band she can hear the faint sound of water lapping. This is what she loves about coke, how you notice everything. The cool, perfect air. How close Pete is standing. The fine red stubble on his cheeks, how it catches the light. She cups her hands around his face. He leans closer, until they are head to head. He puts his mouth on hers. She tastes salt, and pulls away.

"Sorry, I wasn't—"

"Sorry."

"I didn't mean—"

"Me either."

She wonders which of them is sorrier. Which of them loves Roland more.

When they go back in, he's plugged in and standing with the band. "You missed him on 'Dark End of the Street,'" Golita says. Now the band's playing "After Midnight," a slowed-down version, more JJ Cale than Clapton. Two verses in, the singer nods at Roland, and Roland steps up. His shirtsleeves are rolled back. This is his moment, and Addie wonders if he'll break out, burn it up, play some scorching lead, something truly incendiary, even though incendiary isn't what the song calls for. The song is about what's going to happen *after* midnight. In the song, midnight isn't here yet.

Roland knows. He holds back, plays it spare. Long, slow notes with plenty of space in between. It sounds like the front end of a thunderstorm, when the first rain begins to hit the pavement: those slow, fat, hard drops just before the whole sky comes crashing down.

Dear Byrd,

I would like to tell you your father and I loved each other. Maybe we did; maybe love is the right word, though it's not one we ever used. What I can tell you is, he trusted me. He let me see the purest part of him, the music part.

Trust is a sweet thing, and fragile. I was not always as careful with your father's as I should have been.

Sandalwood

A cold, bright Saturday morning in Greensboro. Warren Finch is brewing a pot of chamomile tea for his favorite client, who is seated at the kitchen table with her hands folded in front of her. Her long red hair is pulled back. Her face is golden in the sunlight through the Indian-print curtain. A calendar of Hindu deities hangs on the wall behind her. February is Shiva, god of creation and destruction.

"What do I smell?" she asks.

"Incense," Warren says. "Sandalwood."

The smell reminds him of India, where everywhere, always, there was the smell of burning. Burning sandalwood, burning hashish, burning opium, burning bodies on the ghats at Benares.

"It smells like burnt toast," Addie says.

"I burned my toast, but that was yesterday." He pours their tea into china cups—his mother's wedding pattern, white with yellow roses. He sets the cups on a tray, carries the tray to the table and sets it down stiffly. Getting started is always awkward, a little like striking up a love affair, Warren imagines. The trick is to be both casual and purposeful. He has found with clients that chamomile helps, gentles things.

He serves Addie her tea and offers her half a candy bar. "For this kind of reading, I usually like to have both parties present."

"The other party is in California," she says.

"I know. I'm just saying." He wishes his voice weren't so nasal. People always think he's complaining when in fact it is his practice, in readings and in all things, to remain neutral. To live his life without attachments, to be as a still pond (an *empty* pond, the Buddha would have said, but that's not so picturesque), brilliant as glass, without a ripple. No emotion, no desire—except the one wish, for a different voice, one that could express him perfectly. A deep, resonant, comforting voice that he could wrap around his clients like a coat.

"What's this candy?" Addie says. "It tastes like coconut."

"Bean curd. It's the Indian version of a Mounds bar. Believe it or not, it's called a Barfy."

Addie laughs. Warren laughs. Laughter is good, an auspicious beginning.

"So," he says, "what can I tell you? Which aspects of the relationship are unclear?"

"All aspects. I don't even know what to call the relationship, much less what to do about it."

"What to do, what to do," Warren says, trying to sound lighthearted. "That's the Leo in you, wanting to do, never content simply to be." As a rule, he isn't attracted to Leos—too outward-manifesting. But Addie is an unusual Leo, with three planets in Virgo. She is powerful but doesn't feel her power. She's capable without knowing it.

"He needs to be in L.A. for his music," she says. "I've been thinking about going back. Maybe staying awhile. You keep saying I should travel."

"You don't mean move? Give up your place here? Your job?"

Warren has long been in the habit of stopping in the Readery on his nightly walks. The store is only two blocks away, in a once-fine Victorian house. A calm, welcoming place, full of lamplight and the tapioca smell of old books. Warren doesn't much care for reading himself; his mind is too full already. But he likes to be around other people reading. He likes sitting on a lumpy sofa, drinking tea, listening to pages turn. He likes watching Addie at her square oak desk, an old teacher's desk, wrapping books in clear plastic jackets. She works slowly, meditatively, laying the books open to measure them, folding the jackets down to size. Sometimes, for the smaller books, cutting the jackets. She handles the books tenderly, a glow of utter devotion on her face.

She lives in an apartment on the top floor. Her window has a yellow lace curtain, always a vase of flowers on the sill.

"Travel doesn't necessarily mean move," he tells her. "It can, but it doesn't have to."

He himself is recently home from India. He went traveling as a sort of purification ritual, a way of renouncing his dependence on material comforts, of escaping the numbing day-in-day-outness of life in Greensboro. He wanted a spiritual adventure. He wanted to be able to hear the voice of God if God should speak to him. It's when you're between places, he has always believed, on your way from somewhere to somewhere else, that you're most likely to hear God, because that's when you're most alert. Take Moses. When Moses came upon God in the burning bush he was on his way out of Egypt—fleeing, in fact, after killing a man. God said to Moses, "Go home. Go back to Egypt and take care of your people."

In India, Warren put on orange robes and followed sadhus. He traipsed through streets where skinny men squatted over open gutters and girls skipped along kicking up dust with their bare feet, bells on their ankles tinkling insanely. He sat in an ashram listening to flies he was not allowed to swat. He braved the crowds in Benares to wash his feet in the holy filth of the Ganges. It was there, finally, in that strange, bright, teeming, burning place, that God spoke to him. And, surely not a co-incidence, God told him the same thing he'd told Moses: "Go home. Go home and take care of your mother, Warren. She doesn't know who you are, but she doesn't have anyone else to love her."

So Warren returned to Greensboro. To clean, tree-lined streets and the conveniences of his mother's house—his house now. His bathtub, his gas range, his teakettle. He returned to his clients, some of whom didn't even realize he'd been away, and to his day job in the insurance office. Now, every evening after work, true to the promise he made to God, he stops in the nursing home to read tarot cards for his mother.

"What's this one?" she'll ask. "This one is pretty."

"The Two of Cups," Warren will say. "It's about connecting. About healing broken relationships."

"And what's *this* one? What are these big gold things they're holding?"

"The Two of Cups. Those are cups, Mother."

You don't have to go to India to know death in the midst of life, to hear the sound of silence behind the quickening pulse, to know the nothingness at the core of all being.

"I don't think you came here to talk about moving," he says to Addie. "Where you live, where he lives, that's just geography."

Addie knots her hands. "We have history," she says. "Not a completely nice history, to be honest. But we're connected in a way I've never been connected to anyone else. When I was with him this time, I felt that. I felt like I was *with* him. Like my showing up in his life again after so many years had filled in some missing piece."

Poor Addie, Warren thinks. Getting involved with a Gemini. A mental, moony Gemini—exactly the sort of man who would appeal to her.

"What I can tell you," he says evenly, "is that you aren't going to be able to figure him out. That's the whole point of the relationship for you."

"How can not figuring somebody out be the point of a relationship?"

"Look." Warren shows her Roland's birth chart. "Your friend has no Earth in his chart. Not a trace. In fact there's no Earth in the composite chart, despite your three planets in Virgo." He lays her birth chart on the table alongside the composite. "Roland epitomizes everything you're afraid of. He's the mystery, the unknown. His sun is in the twelfth house of the relationship, the house of mystery. Which means that, to you, he will always be unknowable. Your magical mystery man. That's his role."

Addie studies the charts. "One night he played in a bar," she says, delicately lifting her teacup from its saucer. "I was at a table with his friends and they were telling me how he was the most natural, open, out-there person they'd ever met, and I wanted to say to them, *Really? How do you know?* Because I'm never sure what he's thinking."

"His friends have a different configuration with him than you do. They experience him on a more surface level. On that level he's very direct. But you have a deeper connection, more of a soul-mate connection. Soulful playmates."

"He's been calling me. He forgets the time difference and calls in the middle of the night, when I'm asleep. We don't always talk. Sometimes he just plays his guitar and I listen. He's amazing, even when he's wasted."

"He affects people in powerful ways," Warren says, "though he may not realize it. His Gemini energy makes him so scattered that he's a bit of a mystery even to himself. Capricorn in his seventh house: he needs somebody solid, responsible. He doesn't have much of that in his own life so he has to get it from somebody else."

"Like me."

"Your moon is falling in the fourth house, the house of security and family and rootedness, so yes, you'd be providing that part of the relationship."

"While he's off somewhere being mysterious."

Her wistfulness makes him want to lay his hand on hers. But that would be a breach of ethics.

"You've got Libra on your seventh house cusp," he continues. "Neptune's there, too, which means you're also a great romantic idealist. But you tend to delude yourself by projecting your ideals onto a particular person when in fact that idealism is something more magical about life itself. The more you tap the mystery in yourself, the less weightiness your relationships will have."

He studies her for some sign that his reading is touching on the truth. Almost always, the answers people come to him for are truths they carry inside themselves. His job is to help them uncover what they already know. When a reading rings true, it registers visibly—a change in posture, a flicker in the eyes. Some people get hungry.

Addie is nodding. She has folded her arms across her waist and is rocking back and forth.

"Are you okay?" Warren asks.

"I'm sorry," she says. "I'm feeling a little sick. I think I need your bathroom."

Up on the Roof

Roland is making a picnic. He has never made a picnic for anyone. It's not even a word he uses: *picnic*.

On his counter, blueberry smoothies and crinkle-cut fries from his favorite stand on the beach, plus everything from his kitchen: a can of peaches, half a bottle of white Zinfandel, and two hardboiled eggs, which he peels and mashes into a bowl with salt and pepper. Then there's the barbecue Addie brought with her from North Carolina: hickory-smoked shoulder meat sliced thin, packed on dry ice in her little travel cooler. Slaw, too, and sauce, the thin red tomatoey kind they grew up on. You can't get sauce like this in California.

So much food. A feast, a corn-you-fucking-copia. That's how Addie makes him feel. Rich, generous, overflowing. Like that Bible story where all of a sudden there's plenty of fish and bread to go around. One day he's racking his brain over how to scrape up rent, even thinking he should move Elle back in, the next he's making a picnic.

Loaves and fishes, baby.

It's a warm, gusty February afternoon and they're going to spend it on the roof because Addie has never eaten on a roof. They're going to sit in the sun and eat their picnic and drink their wine and look down on the ocean. When the time comes he will kiss her. She likes being kissed, gives him her mouth full and open, like a flower, one he remembers from home but can't remember the name of. Something with soft, damp petals.

She's swishing around him like a nervous cat, singing that song, "Up on the Roof," by James Taylor or Joni Mitchell or Carole King, one of the people she listens to. He should learn the song so that next time, if there is a next time, he can play it for her the way it ought to sound, jazzy and light—the way you feel when you're on a roof.

He packs the food in his gym bag, the peaches and eggs and smoothies and fries and wine and barbecue. He strips the orange blanket off the sofa bed. Then they climb out the window and up the metal ladder, past the fourth floor—only one flight, but in the wind, carrying their picnic, it feels like more. An *outing*, his mother would call it. Addie goes first, clinging to the rail. A warm breeze is blowing. Her cotton skirt balloons above him; he can see her legs all the way up to her lace panties. Her legs are like stalks, thin and straight and pale. No one in L.A. has legs so pale.

"Roland," she says, her red hair whipping around her head, "if I let go, will you catch me?"

"Sure, baby."

He isn't in love with her. Nobody's talking about love. But if she fell, yes, he would catch her, because she believes he could. She has known him forever and trusts him anyway, and for that he would give her everything. His groceries, his coke if he had any, his roof, his big warm California sky, his ocean.

———

The picnic does not turn out as he's planned.

Addie sits stiff as a queen on the orange blanket, nibbling at her sandwich, now and then flapping her hand in the air to shoo a swooping gull. If she'd just finish eating, the bird would leave her alone. He doesn't know why she's taking such tiny bites, why she chews and chews and chews, unless it's to avoid talking. She's too quiet, not her usual chatterbox self.

He tries pouring wine into her cup and she stops him.

"What are those mountains?" she asks.

"The Santa Monicas."

"They look like elephants."

"Elephants?"

"It's a Hemingway story," she says. She sounds impatient, irritated with him. "'Hills Like White Elephants.' Except those hills aren't white, they're sort of brownish-gray. Taupe."

"*I* read a book," he says. "I saw a show on public TV about John Steinbeck and the next day I went out and got *Of Mice and Men*. Fucking blew me away. I loved that guy Lenny." What he doesn't say, what he's afraid to say, is that he watched the show and read the book *for her*.

"The one you ought to read," she says, "is *The Grapes of Wrath*. The greatest road book ever written."

"Isn't it like ten thousand pages long?"

She squints at the horizon. "Those hills don't really look like elephants."

He opens the peaches and they eat them out of the can. "Last one's yours," he offers, but she pushes the spoon away.

"The Hemingway story," she says, "is about a girl who gets pregnant. She and her boyfriend are trying to decide what she should do."

"What do they decide?" He's being polite. Why the hell is she still talking about this story?

"Nothing, Roland," she says. "Nothing. I'm pregnant."

"Oh," he says. "*Oh.*" Fuck. Of course. *A girl who gets pregnant.* That explains everything—her nervousness, her moodiness. Her not-drinking. He can't believe he didn't figure it out himself. Even her coming back so soon. Of course she would think she had to tell him in person; that's Addie. Dutiful, pale, pregnant Addie.

He imagines her packing for her trip. Choosing what to wear. Picking out the story she would use.

If only he were a reader.

She's starting to cry now, but not hard. He puts his arm around her. "It's okay, baby," he says. "Don't worry, it'll be okay. Addie, look at me." He hands her one of the paper towels they're using as napkins. "That story," he says, "how does it come out?"

"It's Hemingway. It *doesn't* come out."

He pulls her closer and presses her head into his shoulder. Her face soaks his shirt. He doesn't care. He isn't thinking about himself, not yet. It's too soon; he doesn't need to think that far ahead. "It's okay," he says, keeping his voice deep and even. "Just tell me what you want me to do. Tell me, and I'll do it." He has no idea what this means, for himself or for her, but he likes the sound of it. Solid, convincing, strong. Stronger than he has ever been.

Tell me and I'll Do It

Addie's phone wakes her up.

"How you feeling, baby?"

"Tired, Roland. I've never been so tired."

The next night he forgets again and calls at midnight, her time. "How you feeling?"

"Please, Roland, you have to stop calling so late. I'm so tired I could die."

"I'm sorry."

He calls at ten. "Did you get the money I sent?"

"You didn't send it," she says. "Golita did. You told her?"

"Golita is family," he says. "She's like my sister."

"Your sister never liked me."

"Golita's okay."

"I sent it back," she says. A check from Golita for a hundred dollars, less than half the cost of the procedure, and a sticky note in Golita's handwriting, "Good luck." Roland hadn't even addressed the envelope himself.

He calls at seven. She's in the middle of supper. "Please stop calling," she says. She isn't even sleepy this time. "Please just stop."

Someone has to drive her to and from the clinic. It's a requirement. She considers calling Shelia, though they've talked only once or twice since Shelia's twins were born. But this is one secret she doesn't want Shelia to know. It isn't the abortion; it's Roland. She doesn't want Shelia to know she's been with him again. She especially doesn't want Shelia to know that being with him was her idea.

She calls the professor. "It's the least you can do," she tells him.

He comes for her in his Toyota. He's wearing a black cap and sunglasses, like a character in a movie. Sometimes he's such a joke she can't help but love him.

"Do you know how to get there?" she asks.

He nods.

It's a cold, blustery March morning. White pear blossoms whip through the air like snow, a spring blizzard. On the sidewalk outside the clinic, half a dozen men are holding signs. They aren't walking up and down the way you're supposed to on a picket line. They seem frozen in place. Their signs are big white posters with red magic marker letters, the exact same red on every poster, like they all got together in somebody's basement.

"Don't they have jobs?" the professor says.

Addie knows she's supposed to hate them. But they're nothing to her. Standing out in the weather in their wool jackets, too cold to move, they're not even an inconvenience.

Someone should take them coffee, she thinks.

Kerouac's Girlfriend

Roland stands at his bathroom mirror shaving off his mustache. The mirror keeps fogging over. He wipes it with the side of his hand.

The bathroom feels smaller when he's alone. The whole apartment does. Crowded and stale. Nothing nice, just him and his stuff. Dirty clothes, dirty towels, dirty magazines.

When he was on the road he used to daydream about places he might end up. None of them looked like this. This place could be anybody's. *He* could be anybody.

Who can blame Addie for not wanting his kid.

She wouldn't even take money from him, even after he talked it out of Golita. Golita insisted on writing the check herself. "I give you cash, you'll just put it up your nose," she said.

Today is the day. It's happening now, while he shaves. No, fuck, it happened hours ago—he keeps forgetting the time difference. By now it's done.

Kerouac's girlfriend had an abortion. Kerouac wrote about her in *Desolation Angels*. Kerouac's girlfriend's name was Joyce, but Kerouac changed it to Alyce in the book. Back then, abortions were illegal. Nineteen fifty-six—the year Roland was born, and Addie.

He splashes water on his face and checks his reflection. Clean face, clean start. Like nothing's happened yet.

He pictures Addie in a hospital gown, lying on a table, her thin white arms and legs. Is she scared?

Maybe he'll write her a song. Call it "Desolation Angel."

Love, Stay, Keep

The clinic has certain people for certain things. One hands you pills in a paper cup. Another escorts you from room to room: the paperwork room, the changing room, the ultrasound room, small and dark. The lab, all bright lights and needles. The counseling room with windows and potted plants. The procedure room. Finally, the recovery room like a big beauty salon, with magazines and soothing music and reclining chairs lined up in two long rows and a smiling, pink-cheeked woman who walks around serving graham crackers and ginger ale. "More?" she asks. "More?" If kindness could be eaten and drunk, it would taste like graham crackers and ginger ale.

The first couple of rooms—paperwork, changing—are nothing, except the gown Addie has to put on is an insult, a thin blue plastic thing that clings to her skin and crackles when she moves and makes her hair electric.

The ultrasound room is where she comes face to face with what she's doing. She's on a table and a nurse comes in and rubs warm Vaseline on her belly and glides a camera over her. "Show me," she says, and the nurse points to a spot on a black-and-white TV screen. The spot is gray and smaller than a baby bird. Which is how Addie tries to think of him in the beginning: as a bird, something that doesn't belong in her, a mistake, all blind and gray and no feathers. She wonders what others see when they look at the screen, what images they conjure up to fool themselves. She wonders why the clinic, which has people for everything else, doesn't have a person to help with this. A useful-metaphor woman in a nice blue smock and crepe-soled shoes.

Or maybe that's the job of the clinic counselor, the one with potted plants. She sits them down, Addie and two others, a nervous high school girl and a bored twenty-year-old, and asks a few questions to make sure they've come here of their own free will. Then she gives a speech that's supposed to make them feel brave and wise and strong.

"Is there anything else you need to talk about?" she asks them.

The high school girl wants to know if she'll be able to go to the basketball game Friday night. The twenty-year-old says she's been through this before and knows the drill. Addie says nothing. What can she say? Thirty-two and still no readier to be a mother than they are.

"Will it hurt?" the high school girl asks.

"No," the twenty-year-old says.

Why not, Addie thinks. *Don't we deserve at least a little pain?*

In the procedure room, she lies on a table with her feet in stirrups and stares at the chipped polish on her toenails. Mystic Mauve, the color she wore to California to tell Roland.

"Don't move," the doctor says. "I can't do this if you move."

She's shivering; she can't help it. She's cold. Her gown is so thin. She twists her head to find the nurse. "Can I please have a blanket?" she asks. "A sheet, anything?"

"Right back," the nurse says, and disappears out of the room in her silent white shoes, leaving Addie alone with the doctor. Addie tries not to look at him, at his red-rimmed eyes constantly blinking, or the acne scars on his face. She pictures him as a teenager—unpopular, afraid of girls, the shy boy at the dance. Even now, he doesn't make small talk, no "What kind of work do you do?" or "Have you always lived in North Carolina?" or "How about this weather?" Nothing to take her mind off what he's doing. His white coat has a dark fleck on the pocket. Addie tries not to look.

She tries not to look at the tube he is holding.

The sun was brighter that day than she had ever seen it. Everything shone. They sat on Roland's roof and Roland put his arm around her and he was warm, he made her warm, and she wanted to believe, she almost did, that warm could be enough.

"Don't worry," he said, and rubbed his hand up and down her back. "It'll be okay."

He was kind. He didn't say anything wrong. The problem wasn't what he said, but what he left out. Things Addie thought he might say, even if they weren't true, he didn't. He didn't say *love*. He didn't say *stay*. Or *keep*.

"Keep your feet in the stirrups," the doctor says, blinking. "Keep your knees apart. Relax, please."

Finally the nurse comes back with a flannel sheet. She drapes it over Addie, tucks it around her bare arms as if she were the child. "There," she says. "Better?"

mistake

So much they didn't tell her.

They told her to expect spotting, wear pads, call if the bleeding got heavy. They told her to expect cramping. Take ibuprofen, not aspirin. Use a hot water bottle.

They didn't tell her her breasts would continue to swell and ache and leak.

They didn't tell her about the insatiable hunger, the strange cravings. Sharp cheddar cheese. Egg salad sandwiches—plain, no lettuce—on untoasted white bread. Peanut M&Ms. She eats them by the jumbo bag until she is sick.

She keeps gaining weight. More than can be explained by the M&Ms.

They didn't tell her she would cry over everything, every song on the radio, every line in every book, every movie. She goes to matinees, romantic comedies—*Say Anything, See You in the Morning*—and comes out of the dark theater with her face puffy and wet, her eyes red. People waiting to buy tickets stare at her, puzzled—*are we in the right line?*

It's hormones, she thinks. Hormones and grief. Yes, grief—she has had a loss. That she chose it makes it no less a loss.

They didn't warn her about the nightmares. Every night, a vivid, lifelike dream in which it falls to her to rescue some helpless creature from sure death. A kitten stalked by lions. A nest of robin's eggs invaded by a snake. A child on a banana-seat bicycle pedaling into the path of an oncoming train. Impossible situations, beyond her; even in her sleep she knows it. Somehow she always wakes up a split second before the catastrophe, always in a cold sweat.

This, she has always imagined, is how it must feel to be a mother. Terrifying. Numbingly exhausting. She is so tired her whole body hurts but she is afraid to sleep, afraid of what may happen to the next poor dream-creature entrusted to her.

Finally she makes an appointment with her doctor.

"Sounds like you're pregnant," says the nurse who takes her blood pressure and charts her symptoms. The nurse has round brown perpetually stunned eyes.

"Impossible," Addie says. She had not intended to confess her abortion to anyone, even her doctor. Certainly not to this Bambi-eyed nurse.

"Have you had a period since?" the nurse asks.

"No, but—" Even as she protests, she knows the nurse is right. Her body knows.

The test confirms it. The doctor doesn't try to explain how this could have happened. She refers Addie to an obstetrician; Addie insists on a woman. No more men, not after the pockmarked clinic doctor who botched her abortion. She would like to sue him, but for what? Unnecessary pregnancy? Wrongful life?

The obstetrician is tall and grandmotherly—gray hair, a big rosy face, blue eyes so pale they seem full of light. There are hand-knit booties on the stirrups of her examining table.

"You have an unusual uterus," she tells Addie. She has a hint of a foreign accent—Scottish? "It tips at an odd angle. You have a blind spot where a baby can hide."

Which, she says, explains how the baby survived. It wasn't the clinic doctor's fault. It wasn't anyone's fault. Sometimes abortions ("a-*bar*-shins") fail. Just like sometimes birth control fails. Sometimes, against all odds, babies happen.

"Your baby is perfectly fine. See?" On the sonogram screen, the baby lies in profile. The doctor traces the hands, heart, head, facial features.

"It's smiling," Addie says.

"Would you like to know the sex?"

"The sex," Addie says. Somehow this seems unfair—she didn't know the sex before; why should she get to know now?

"Some do, some don't," the doctor says. "There's no right or wrong."

Still, she's tired of surprises. "I guess so," she says. "Sure."

The doctor smiles; her teeth are crooked but bright. She points out the baby's privates in the shape of a small turtle ("tairtle")—the shell of testicles, the tiny peeking-out penis-head. "A boy," she says. "A healthy boy."

"Healthy."

"Yes. He wasn't harmed, if that's your worry. All it did, the procedure, was make a nice clean place for him to settle into. A perfect little nest. You have nothing to fret about."

Nothing, Addie thinks, *except what do I do now?*

She tries telling Roland about the baby. Twice. Once in June, but his phone has been disconnected. She calls again in July and a woman answers.

"Hello?" The woman's voice is guarded, timid, like she's been waiting for bad news. "Hello?"

"Is Roland there?"

"Can I say who's calling?"

Addie doesn't ask the woman's name; she doesn't have to. Elle. Elle who forgot her blouse in Roland's closet. Elle who has come to his rescue—again—with rent money. Elle: betrayed, humiliated, but still hanging on, wondering if she's done the right thing moving back in.

"Never mind," Addie says. "Wrong number. My mistake."

Notice by Publication

The Guilford County Department of Social Services is in an ugly brick building. The social worker assigned to Addie, a woman named Janet, has plain brown hair, washed-out skin, and tired eyes. They are starting the paperwork for the adoption. Addie is sitting in a wooden chair with wide flat arms, like a witness chair.

"Your full name," Janet says.

"Adela Claire Lockwood."

On a file cabinet under Janet's window is an African violet full of blue blossoms and fat, furry leaves, and next to it, a picture of two children—a boy and a girl—in a white frame. The children are plain like Janet. Obedient-looking, sitting still for the camera. They'll be home from school by now, Addie imagines—it's late afternoon. Waiting for their mother to finish up with her last client and come make them dinner. By the time Janet gets home they will have the table set.

"Father's name?"

"My father?"

"The child's."

"Roland." Addie stops. Is it really necessary to involve him?

"Last name?"

"I don't know."

"You don't remember or you never knew?"

Roland would sign the papers, of course. But does she want to ask him? He will tell people. He'll tell his friends. Golita. Elle. What if Elle says to him, "No, Roland, let me raise him"? Unlikely. But what if he tells his mother and his mother says, "No, let *me* raise him"?

Maybe if he'd sent the money for the abortion himself. Or offered to come and be with her, even if he couldn't afford to. Or called her afterwards, even though she told him not to.

Maybe if there were no Elle.

Maybe if his chart contained any Earth.

"Never knew," Addie says.

"You're sure."

"I'm sure."

Janet follows procedure. Using the bits and pieces Addie claims to remember (some of them true), she puts together a legal notice and publishes it in a small, cheap Los Angeles County newspaper. The notice says that a child was conceived on or about December 31, 1988, in Venice Beach. That "Roland, no last name given" is the child's putative father. That the child is to be relinquished for adoption in North Carolina and that "the aforesaid Roland" has the right to claim paternity, which will entitle him to notice of any hearings involving the child. Otherwise his rights will be terminated.

Maybe there are people who sit around drinking coffee and checking the local papers to make sure nobody's having their baby. Addie doubts it. Anyway, she's sure Roland is not one of them.

Summer 1989

Dear—

What to call you? Almost-child? One who has taken root in me and won't let go? One who might have been mine? Could still be, if I were brave enough?

But I'm not. I can't be the mother you deserve. I know this in the way other women know they're meant to be mothers. I know from everything I have ever been or dreamed or wanted.

You will not read this letter, which is the only reason I'm brave enough to write it. You will not know what you went through to get here. Already you are braver than I will ever be.

I promise to take better care of us from now on. No more red M&Ms, even if the government says they're safe. No more coffee or pink wine. No more coke, even if I knew where to get it (I suppose I could ask one of the late-night talkers in the bookstore where I work, but I don't want that kind of intimacy with any of those people; I don't want that kind of intimacy with anyone else ever again). No more cigarettes.

You are resilient. (I would call you lucky but that would go too far.) My doctor says you are healthy, all your parts intact and in the right place.

You are a secret I share only with my doctor. And with my boss, who wants to know why I'm getting so big and private and morose, why I can't be around people.

Dear creature who has taken up residence in me,

If I were going to keep you I would be thinking of names. I would be shopping for hats and blankets and sleepers and onesies and tiny pull-on pants in the softest eggshell blue. I'd pick out a bassinet, a stroller, a changing table, a swing. I would be learning to install a car seat and administer CPR.

This is what I do instead:

During the day, when the store is closed to custom- ers, when it's just you and me, I read to you. Lately I've been reading from the new catalog I'm working on, Books About Books. *No matter how much you've been kicking— you are a ferocious kicker—my voice settles you. "Entry number thirty. Aldis, Henry G.* The Printed Book. *Cam- bridge. Cambridge University Press, nineteen forty-one, second edition, yellow cloth, one hundred forty-two pages. Slightly soiled and sunned, short tear at spine head, bind- ing good, text very good. Douglas C. McMurtrie's copy with his signature. Twenty-five dollars."*

My boss, I'll call him J.D., taught me about books. He taught me vocabulary, like "foxing" for the brown spots old books get, the same as old-age spots on people. He showed me worm trails—when a worm eats through a book it leaves a little path from one page to the next. He says you can sometimes find the body of the worm, but I never have.

J.D. goes around in lumberjack shirts and has an odd, ripe smell, like turmeric. He's always humming old songs, the Doors, Moody Blues. A refrigerator of a man, he hums without knowing he's humming.

All summer he has been taking care of me in his big, easy, pretend-not-to way. He's going to the grocery store, it's no trouble to pick up a few extra things, what do I need? He has to run errands, he can drive me to my appointments. I love riding in his van—an Econoline like the one your father drives, but silver, not blue. I love sitting up high, looking down on people in cars. I love FM radio, the thick lull of sleepy voices, like they're speaking through water. The way my voice sounds to you, maybe.

Sometimes on Sundays J.D. and I drive out to the country to a lake with a sandy beach. We don't know anyone there. We go wading together, like a little family. I let J.D. touch my belly and you do your stunts. He says you feel fluttery, like a trapped bird. Not just any bird, I say. One with strong wings. A crow or a raven.

Sometimes I wish I loved J.D. I wish I could ever love the right person.

Dear creature who gives me heartburn and presses on my bladder and won't let me sleep on my side,

Why do I write you letters you will never read? Because I want a record of this time with you. Because soon I will have nothing else to show for it. Once upon a time, I was pregnant. A baby grew in me. I read to him. Once upon a time, I was a mother.

Dear baby,

You love the Talking Heads song about staying up late. I dance and you dance inside me. What a change of pace, you must be thinking, from the slow, sad songs I usually make myself miserable with. Judee Sill, Joni Mitchell, Carole King. You like them too, by the way, especially Carole King.

I wonder how much music you absorb. Years from now, when you hear "So Far Away," will it spark some memory of this time? It's a memorable song, mostly because of the bass line, which has in it every bit of unrootedness and longing there ever was.

Dear baby,

The doctor who will deliver you is tall and confident, with strong hands that never sweat. Her hands make me feel safe. I noticed them when we first met, when she took out her magic paper disk and spun it to tell me when you would arrive—September 23. She has practical fingernails, trimmed short and polished with clear lacquer. She wears a simple silver wedding band on her left hand and a mother's ring on her right, with five different-colored stones. I want to ask about her children. Where are they? I want to ask. Do you miss them?

I'm thinking of my own mother, sitting at home, lonesome for her children (I haven't visited all summer; I can't, not in the shape I'm in), uselessly dreaming of grandchildren. I sometimes think the hardest part of giving you up will be knowing that I am taking you away from her.

Dear baby,

There are days when the thought of bringing you into the world so that you can be someone else's child is almost too much. I'm like some soul-flattened character in a Kafka story or one of those absurdist plays I used to love.

People talk about the kind of commitment it takes to be a mother. No one talks about how hard it is to hold onto the decision not *to be a mother when there's a baby growing in you.*

My doctor has been careful not to weigh in on my decision. She only tests and measures and prescribes vitamins and tries to keep us healthy.

J.D. tells me I'm doing a beautiful thing and that I should not lose sight of that. I wish I could believe him. Then I could write you letters filled with platitudes about how everything will work out for the best, instead of letters I can never let you read.

II.

Born

The Infant Survivor

September 14, 1989. Parkertown on a Friday evening. Rows of wooden houses, windows squinting like drunks in the late sun. Women in dresses propped in open doorways. Men inside laughing, glass jars clanking. Every now and then a whiff of reefer. Children and dogs running circles in dirt yards. Tonight the children will stay up late while the grownups get high, because it's the weekend, no school tomorrow.

This is the rundown, furniture-mill part of Carswell, home to bootleggers and drug dealers. It has its own history: the part of town that burned in the Fourth of July fire of 1910. The mill had let out early for the holiday, and in the excitement somebody forgot the oily rags in the finish room. That night, after the barbecue and watermelon and sack races, after the gospel band and the fireworks, everybody went to bed so full and tired and happy and slept so hard that no one heard the explosion, or if they did, they thought it was just more fireworks. Flames shot out the roof of the finish room, fanned across the mill, and rolled through Parkertown—all the little wood shacks, the yards full of trash, the sleeping families. Twenty-five houses burned to the ground and everyone in them died except one child, a boy, Bobo Hairston, who was flung out a window and into a neighbor's yard, where he landed in a patch of soft dirt the neighbor had shoveled up for a garden that never got planted.

A miracle, the firemen called him. The miraculous infant survivor.

Bobo was sent away to the colored orphanage, grew up, married a girl from the home, and brought her back to Carswell to start a family. He got a job at the Fifty-Fifty on Cotton Grove Road where he bagged and delivered groceries until the store closed in 1972.

Bobo's wife is dead now, and he is nearly blind, but whenever anyone asks, "How you doing, Bobo," he still says what he's always said. "Lucky to be here." People ask just to hear him say it, like putting quarters in a jukebox.

The spot where Bobo landed is now covered with a house— small, weather-beaten, rough as a scab. There are houses where all the old houses burned. They look like the old ones used to. Like kindling.

Music wafts out of open doorways. Sultry voices—Luther Vandross, Anita Baker. In one doorway a crusty-faced boy huddles against his mother and stares wide-eyed at the street, where a white woman is passing by—a thin, tight-lipped, very white woman. She keeps to the middle of the street, but the street is narrow and the yard so shallow the boy could count the woman's eyelashes if he could count. She walks like somebody in a parade, stiff, stamping her feet. She's carrying a box of Kentucky Fried Chicken in both hands. Her hair is twisted in a bun, black hair with a thick spiral of silver. She is such a surprise the dogs forget to bark; the dogs don't even go after the smell of chicken. The little boy yanks on his mother's skirt. "What you *want*," his mother says, smacking his hand.

He points at the white woman's hair. "Swirly," he says.

That night Claree gets a long-distance call from Sam, who's in Arizona, visiting his wife's family. Margaret's parents live in the desert outside Tucson. Claree has never been to Tucson. She's never seen a desert. She has never been outside North Carolina. She thinks of deserts not as places but as blanks between places.

Sam is talking about some cactus-tree park Margaret's parents took them to. He's talking fast, like he's afraid of running out of breath. "They're fifty feet tall, some of them. They look almost human. Like giants."

"They aren't real trees," Claree says.

"What?"

"Cactuses. They aren't real trees." She lights a cigarette and wishes he weren't having such a good time. She has been losing him since the day he was born. "Ca*cti*, I mean."

Margaret's parents live in a fake-adobe house, Claree has seen pictures, with a swimming pool and a patio and a built-in barbecue grill. They're all sitting by the pool now. It's earlier there. The sun is just going down. Claree pictures them in lounge chairs, Margaret and her parents drinking their beer out of glasses, snacking on corn chips and salsa, watching their big Western sunset, and Sam sitting off to one side, talking on the phone, saying things he wants them to hear even though they're pretending not to listen. In the background, Margaret's father laughs his deep, confident, businessman laugh. He impressed everyone at the wedding—so relaxed, so smooth with jokes, so tanned. Claree pictures him in expensive leather sandals. Getting up to throw steaks on the grill. She knows Sam will have to hang up soon.

"Your father left me at the chicken place this evening," she says.

"He what?"

"He stayed in the car while I went in to get our dinner. When I came out, he wasn't there. Apparently he thought he could slip over to the VFW for another drink and get back before I missed him, but then he forgot about me. I waited and waited, but he never came. I had to walk home through Parkertown."

"Why didn't you call somebody?"

"I wasn't scared. I was too mad to be scared. I got home with our chicken and there was his car, in the Davenports' front yard, parked right in the middle of their big pink camellia. And him still sitting behind the wheel."

"You should have called somebody. You should have called Addie."

"She's an hour away."

"Forty minutes."

"She doesn't want to be bothered." She is trying not to let him hear how let down she is, and not only by Addie. "You know, she hasn't been home all summer? Every time we talk it's a different excuse. Busy at work, sick with a cold, something. She won't say what's really wrong, but I know. It's your father. I think she stays away because of him."

"Is he okay?"

"He's fine. When I got to him he was calm as could be. Sitting in that big bush like he was stopped in traffic, waiting for the light to change."

In a hospital room in Greensboro, the baby is coming.

After eleven hours of contractions, Addie asks for an epidural. The drugs turn her blood to ice water. She starts to shiver. Then the lower half of her goes numb—solid, dentist's-office numb. Then they stretch her legs apart, sit her up, drop the bottom out of the bed and tell her to push.

She pushes.

She can't tell what's happening with the baby because she can't feel anything from her rib cage down, but she pushes anyway, until she thinks the top of her head will explode. For an hour and a half she pushes, until she's running a fever of a hundred and two.

In the end they have to do a C-section. They take her to the operating room and lay her on a narrow table and put clips on her fingers. The doctor leans over and assures her there's nothing to fret about. The doctor's big face looks freshly scrubbed. Her gray hair is tucked into a cap. "You'll feel a twitch," she says, "like when your eye jumps."

Addie can't see what's happening, but when they open her, there is a smell like meat gone bad.

Then someone says, "We've got him."

Addie isn't allowed to hold him because of her incision. The nurse has to hold him up above her draping. The nurse is short, her arms a cradle of fat. "Your son," she says, smiling proudly.

Addie draws in her breath.

Whatever she'd been expecting, it wasn't this. It wasn't *him*. His face isn't shriveled but smooth and pink. His hair is a mat of dark wet feathers. His eyes are fierce. Addie raises her head to kiss him, but misses, and kisses the nurse's hand instead. Then the nurse carries him away. Addie can hear him down the hall, his hungry, hopeless squawking.

She names him Byrd. With a Y, like an open beak.

"This probably isn't the best time to mention it," Sam says to Claree, "but Margaret and I are thinking of moving."

"Where?"

"Out here. Where it's dry. Where I can breathe."

"I don't understand, honey. Plenty of people with asthma live in North Carolina. Isn't your medicine working?"

"Sure, it's working just fine, the steroids and inhalers. Also ruining my liver. Didn't you read the book I sent?"

"I was going to," Claree says. It isn't that she doesn't take Sam's asthma seriously; she just doesn't like to think about it all the time. "What about an air purifier? I've heard there's a new one on the market like they use in hospitals. I've heard it removes dust and moisture and everything."

Sam doesn't answer. Claree knows this silence by heart.

"I just worry you won't be happy in the desert," she says, "with no trees. You love trees. When you were small your favorite place was the woods. We bought that yellow teepee and set it up in the woods, and you and Addie practically moved in. That was before the Davenports bought the lot next door, remember? Remember the summer you found the bird? A robin with a broken wing, and we built a cage for it next to the teepee, and you and Addie spent all summer nursing it, digging up worms and feeding it until it could fly."

"It was a Blue Jay."

She lights another cigarette, sighs into the receiver. "I still think about that lot next door. We should have bought it when we had the chance, before the Davenports cut down your woods."

"Did you know," Sam says, "that most kids whose parents smoke get asthma sooner or later?"

"That can't be true. Where did you hear that?"

"Something like sixty-five percent. It was in the book I sent you."

"Does this book say anything about air purifiers? Because I've heard the new one is supposed to take everything out of the air."

Non—Identifying Information

Dear Byrd,

My social worker, Janet Worry (not her real name), says I should write you letters. She doesn't know I've been writing you all along.

She says a lot of her mothers (that's how she talks, "my mothers") have trouble getting started. Some copy out favorite poems or song lyrics. Some send greeting cards.

"Greeting cards?" I said.

"It's a start," she said.

"What do your mothers write about?" I said.

"Everything," she said, "anything. Sometimes it's easiest to start with the facts, details of the child's birth. Whatever you think your child might like to know. Just be careful to leave out any identifying information."

On the day you were born, J.D. took me to the hospital and went with me to the maternity floor. The carpet in the elevator smelled like iodine. One stop before ours, an orderly got on pushing a woman on a gurney. The woman's *arms were covered with needle bruises. She had a high, weak voice, and she kept asking the orderly, "Why are you doing this, why are you doing this?"*

They took me to a room and put me in a bed and J.D. came in and planted himself in the recliner and turned on the TV, some show about dolphins. I watched him watching. I watched the dolphins in his glasses. The room smelled like him. I felt safe. Then a nurse came in all crisp and efficient and said to him, "Are you the father?"

"The driver," he said.

"Maybe you'd like to wait in the waiting room."

J.D. stood up. He looked like Paul Bunyan. He came and stood over my bed and laid his hand on the top of my head like he had something to tell me. "Let me know how the show comes out," he said.

He waited fourteen hours before they called him to the nursery. Could you see him there, pressing his big face to the glass? He said he knew without asking which one was you. He said you looked like me, sort of, and sort of like the man on the dolphin channel.

Three days later he took me home. He had a present waiting for me, a grab-box from his latest estate sale. Grab-boxes are how the sale companies clear out a person's small, junky items that can't be sold by themselves. Twenty-five, fifty cents, you take your chances. J.D. had gotten me a fifty-cent box. It had a pot of dead chrysanthemums, a glass frog for flower-arranging, a crocheted Kleenex-box cover, three shrimp forks, and a pair of ladies' worn-out terry cloth slippers still attached by a plastic thread. J.D. shoved his big feet in the slippers and tried inching along in them. "Here she is trying to get to the telephone," he said. He wanted to make me laugh, and I wanted to. But I could only picture the old woman from the hospital elevator, the one who kept asking, Why are you doing this?

Dear Byrd,
Dolphins help women have babies, and not just by swimming around on TV screens in hospital rooms.
There's a man in Russia, a famous midwife who delivers babies underwater, in the Black Sea. He says dolphins are attracted to mothers. It's like they know. When a woman gives birth, the dolphins gather around her, smiling the way dolphins do, and lift the baby on their long noses and carry it up to the surface where it can breathe.

Dear Byrd,
When I was growing up there was a strange old man who lived next door to my grandparents. Mr. Junius Beck. When my family went for our Sunday afternoon visits, my brother and I would slip over to Mr. Beck's. He lived in a small white house with artificial flowers stuck in the ground outside the front door, his plastic garden. He would invite us inside and offer us candy hard as fossils. Then he'd take out his family album, a green notebook worn at the edges, and turn to a picture of his wife and infant daughter, who had died years earlier from a gas leak while he was away from home. He had photographed them at their funeral—in the picture, they were lying together in a coffin in their frilly clothes. "Here's Annie Mae and the baby in the corpse," he would say. My brother and I knew better than to laugh at his wrong word. Even as children we knew enough to say, "We're sorry, we're so sorry." The words seemed to work like a drug. Mr. Beck would let out a little sigh, a soft, rumbling sound from deep in his throat. Then

he would close the picture album, set it back on the shelf, pass us the candy jar and let us fill our pockets.

We kept up this creepy Sunday ritual for a long time— months—until our parents learned about it and ordered us not to go back.

I didn't think about Mr. Beck again for years. Not until after you were born.

I was in pain from the surgery. Every part of me felt raw. I had nothing left of you, not even a picture in an album. I had a constant lump in my throat. No one sent get-well cards or brought casseroles because no one knew. I didn't expect or deserve sympathy.

I didn't lure unsuspecting children with candy. But I came to understand why Mr. Beck did. How sad and guilty and lost he must have felt. How he must have craved our pure, sweet, unjudging "I'm sorry"s.

Dear Byrd,

Janet Worry expects me to turn my letters over to her, not keep them in a shoebox on a shelf in my closet. It's an Easy Spirit box, the one my black suede boots came in.

Janet isn't old but she always looks tired, like she isn't quite ready for whatever is happening. On the day you were born, she wore a sleeveless dress to the hospital. I could see powderpuffs of dark hair under her arms. Her dress was wrinkled. The papers she took out of her satchel were wrinkled. She sat on the edge of my bed and petted my arm and said "There, there," like she understood how I felt. Social workers think they know you. They don't want you to tell them things. None of the forms Janet gave me to fill out asked why I was giving you up.

She didn't come to the hospital until after the nurse had taken you away; that was the rule. I asked her if I could see you again to say a proper goodbye. She said that's what the letters were for.

Dear Byrd,

If I were going to send you song lyrics I would choose the song your father played for me the last time I saw him. We were in his apartment, I was packing to leave, and he said there was something he wanted me to hear before I went. I thought he meant something he'd written (he's a musician), but he put on a record by Gladys Knight and the Pips. He set the needle to the last song on side one, "Till I See You Again."

Gladys's voice on the song is sometimes smooth and velvety, sometimes raw and brokenhearted. She is saying goodbye, but not forever. Her friend is leaving but he's coming back. Until he does, she's going to wait for him, dream about him, save up all her love and put her life on hold for him.

Your father danced with me in his kitchen. He leaned me against the counter. We knocked over a glass. It rolled onto the floor and broke, but we didn't stop, we kept dancing, through the key change, through Gladys's call-and-response with the Pips, all the way to the end of the song, when the record began to skip—"again-gain-gain."

Your father gave me the album as a going-away present. On the cover is a picture of a barefoot child looking up at gnarly trees. Your father signed it the same way he'd signed my high school yearbook, with his first and last names, as if I might forget.

Dear Byrd,

You were born in one place but conceived in another, a faraway place near an ocean. There was a man there who swallowed fire. He would light a long stick and put it in his mouth and people would clap and cheer and drop money in his box.

Everybody in that place went around on wheels—skates, skateboards, scooters, bicycles, unicycles. I saw a two-legged dog with wheels where his back legs should have been, his own little built-in chariot.

It almost never rained there. When it did, your father told me, children stayed home from school.

Dear Byrd,

This is what my astrologer says about you: You are a Virgo, with a probing mind and a head for logic. You are older than your years. "Like Tom Sawyer," my astrologer said. "Or was it Huck Finn?"

Your moon is in Aquarius, which means you will feel different from other people, like you don't fit in, which can be a problem because your sun is in Virgo, so you'll want to fit in. (I have a lot of Virgo in me, so this is something I understand.)

Most of your planets are in the western hemisphere, the hemisphere of fate, as opposed to the hemisphere of self-determination. Your life feels like something that happens to you regardless of what you do. This is also true for me. People come into our lives mysteriously and become important in ways we don't understand.

I can guess what you're thinking: why would I confide in an astrologer? I don't even know if he's a good astrologer. He's a thin, ghosty man with gray skin, damp hands, and a voice that cracks. He wears a huge wristwatch and clothes that don't match, plaids with plaids. He is so dour that if he ever smiles his face looks like it's breaking.

But he is trustworthy. I can tell him things and he won't betray me, because he has no one to betray me to. He is the most alone person I know.

Your moon is in the tenth house, which means you have a strong emotional bond with your mother.

"Which mother?" I asked.

"I don't know," he said.

Anything You Love

A thunderstorm follows Bryce to Greensboro. He's driving to his meeting, listening to the radio, some tired country song turned up loud so he can hear it over the thumping windshield wipers. It's a long drive, especially in the rain. He doesn't mind.

Claree once asked him why he didn't go to the meeting in Carswell. He said, are you kidding?

He exits onto Holden Road. The church comes up fast on the left, a brick building in the shape of a triangle. Lutheran.

He is the first to arrive. He turns on the lights in the fellowship hall, a big room in the basement with humming fluorescent lights, waxy floors, painted brick walls, a cross, a plastic tree, and a lectern they don't use because this meeting is open discussion, not speakers. He makes the coffee and sets out Styrofoam cups. He unpacks the literature and spreads it on a table along the wall, props posters on easels, unfolds metal chairs. He likes the sound they make, a gentle *creak creak*. It gives him a sense of purpose. He's been sober nineteen days, his longest stretch yet, and he's craving a sense of purpose. He has never felt so empty. His insides burn.

Gradually the others come in, shake off their umbrellas, pour themselves coffee. They pull their chairs into a circle and wait, talk to each other quietly, their voices steady as the rain outside. Finally Irv looks at the clock and says it's time. A big man, Irv, with a big voice. Retired military. The meeting is supposed to be leaderless but Irv always leads. "Let's open with the Serenity Prayer," he says.

Bryce looks down without closing his eyes. He looks at the circle of shoes. Running shoes, muddy brogans, loafers, Topsiders with curled toes, his own zip-up ankle boots. Sandals, giant leather sandals with black socks—Irv. Bryce has always believed you can judge a man by his shoes. But they aren't supposed to judge in the program. They're supposed to accept and be grateful for each other. In the program, all their thoughts are supposed to be like prayers. Thy socks and thy sandals, they comfort me.

They go through the introductions and the reading of the preamble and the welcome and the steps. Then Irv announces tonight's topic: expectations. He reads a passage out of the Big Book. "Who wants to start the discussion?" he says. "Bryce?" Even though they aren't supposed to call on each other.

Bryce nods. "I'm having trouble with my wife's expectations." The others laugh like he's making a joke. "It hasn't been three weeks and already she's making plans. She talks about how long she's waited to do things other people do. Join the choir. Take square-dance lessons." He looks at the shoes to the left of his. Long white running shoes, narrow as a woman's. Chuck. "She tells me I ought to drop in on our daughter after meetings. We have a daughter in Greensboro. 'Drop in,' she says. Like I'm not the last person on earth my daughter wants to see."

"Remember the reading," Irv says, though they aren't supposed to give advice. "What do we do with expectations?" He looks around the circle.

"Let them go."

"Let them go."

"Let them go."

"They're not mine to let go," Bryce says.

"I don't mean your wife's expectations," Irv says. "Or your daughter's. Yours. Let them go. Live in the present. One day at a time."

They're all watching him. Their faces look worn, ancient.

Something in him relaxes.

At the end of the meeting they all stand up and hold hands and pump their arms and chant: "Keep coming back! It works if you work it, so work it, you're worth it!" Bryce holds Irv's hand, which is meaty and hot, and Chuck's, cool as a bone. The chant is embarrassing. They grin at each other and roll their eyes. This is part of the program, to go through embarrassing motions together so that no one can judge or be judged.

Afterwards he feels light. He feels like celebrating. If he knew where to find a bar in Greensboro he could go out for a drink. Just one, and feel even lighter.

As a child he was small for his age, stunted by asthma, the runt of a litter of five boys.

His ma spent her evenings at prayer meetings and left him with his brothers, who ignored him, and Cicero, who passed out on the couch. When his ma came home she would put Cicero to bed first, then Bryce, like nothing was the matter.

No one else at his school had a father named Cicero. That, plus being small, plus having asthma, plus coming from the mill village, made him a natural target for bullies. He learned two lessons at school. One: Every day would be a new fight. Two: He would always lose.

Dark fall night. A thumbnail moon.

The bookstore where his daughter works is in a nice old house in a neighborhood of nice old houses. He stands on the sidewalk across the street, out of the streetlight, in the fat black shadow of a magnolia tree. He's pretending he belongs here; maybe he lives in one of the houses and his wife doesn't allow him to smoke inside so he's come out for a cigarette before bed. The store's front window gives off a dusky yellow glow. He can see Addie behind the counter inside, talking to a customer. Her red hair is a curtain; he can't see her face, only her hands, fluttering the way they do. Books excite her. She won prizes for reading when she was small—all those silver dollars.

He has always been a little afraid of her. She isn't soft like her mother. She has sharp edges. Sharp green eyes.

One day not long ago he listened in on the extension while she and her mother were talking. "It's a disease," Claree was saying.

"Is that what you call it?" Addie said.

They say in the program that you can't change the past, that your life starts now. But Bryce doubts he can start over with his children. He doubts they will let him. What he needs is a new person, someone who doesn't know him yet, who doesn't know enough to be angry or ashamed. A grandchild. Someone who will give him a chance to be good again, to show there is love in him. Because there is, or there's starting to be. If he can love Irv, he can love anybody.

He drops his cigarette on the sidewalk and grinds it with the toe of his boot. He shoves his hand in his pocket, fingers his new chip. He still can't believe he's in a program where they give poker chips as prizes. Or that getting them matters to him. Addie would laugh. She is stepping out from behind the counter, coming toward the window like she knows he's out here. But he is contained in the shade of the magnolia, safe in the dark.

Invisibly, he waves at her.

He passed his asthma down to his son.

Sam used to get so sick at night he couldn't lie flat. He would sit up in his bed, rocking and creaking his bedsprings and keeping everyone awake. Claree would give him his Primatene spray; she would rub his back with VapoRub; she'd put VapoRub in the humidifier. But there were nights when nothing worked and they had to take him to the hospital. Bryce always drove. He drove as fast as he could.

In the hospital, the lights were so bright they made a noise, a high-pitched whine like a mosquito. Sam had to sit on a metal table in his spaceship pajamas, wheezing, *whee-haw, whee-haw,* while they waited for the doctor. "Don't cry," Bryce would say. "Crying takes too much breath."

Winter, and he's sitting in Addie's apartment.

She's out of coffee, she tells him, but she can make hot chocolate.

"Sure," he says. "Hot chocolate would be good."

She goes to put the kettle on.

Her rooms have flowered wallpaper and everything smells like mothballs. She is like an old lady, except she is young. Thirty-six, thirty-seven? No children, no husband, no boyfriend, according to Claree. She has lived in this apartment forever, and worked in the bookstore downstairs. Maybe she feels safe here. Maybe, for her, safe is enough.

"I'm glad you came," she says, setting their mugs on coasters.

"You are?" He looks at her. "Have you cut your hair?"

"No."

"You look different."

"So do you."

They sip their hot chocolates. All her furniture has slipcovers. She says, "You didn't drive all the way to Greensboro just to see me."

"No." He tells her about his meeting. "I would have dropped by sooner," he says. She asks about the program. How does it work? What do they do at meetings? What are the steps?

It isn't her hair, he realizes. It's her eyes that are different. They aren't hard when she looks at him. Careful, but not hard.

"What was it like to stop?" she says. "Do you miss it?"

"Sure," he says. "It's like giving up anything you love."

"Oh," she says. Her voice, too. There's something new in her voice, something that doesn't dismiss him. "Where are you now?" she says. "Which step?"

"The fourth. I'm taking a personal inventory. Listing good and bad things about myself. Guess which list is longer."

She stares at him, almost smiles. "Remember the time you tried to smoke your pencil?"

"My pencil?"

"Your golf pencil. It was in your cigarette pocket and you pulled it out and stuck it in your mouth and told Sam to light it. And got mad when it wouldn't draw."

He forces a laugh. In her way she is being kind. This can't be the worst thing she remembers.

"Did you need help with the good list?" she says.

"That's not why I came." He's a little irritated—with himself or her, he couldn't say. He finishes his hot chocolate, which is no longer hot.

"You have good taste in clothes," she says. "You've always been a snappy dresser."

"Thanks." He's wearing his navy sweater and brown wool slacks, the zip-up boots.

"You cook. You always made us breakfast on school days—bacon and eggs. Saturdays you grilled chicken. You made your own barbecue sauce."

He wants to say, *Grilling out isn't something you get credit for.*

"You had your picture on a billboard," she says.

"It embarrassed you."

"Everything embarrassed me."

"I'm sorry," he says.

She shrugs.

"No," he says. "Listen to me, Addie. I don't know how to make amends. I'm not that far along yet. But I want you to know I'm sorry."

"You took us for ice cream on Sundays," she says.

Sundays had been his sober days. He remembers hot afternoons in the Tastee Freez parking lot, Addie and Sam in the back seat, their sticky cones dripping on the vinyl, Claree with her hot fudge sundae—no nuts—eating with her tiny spoon as slowly as she could, making hers last long after he'd wolfed down his banana split.

"You can stop now," he says. "This is starting to feel like a eulogy."

It will happen in the spring. At work, at his gray metal desk. He'll open his bottom drawer, take out the lunch Claree has packed for him, a meatloaf sandwich with lettuce and mustard, and feel a stab of pain in his shoulder. At first he won't want to believe what's happening, but he will know. The body knows. He will reach for the picture on his desk, an old family snapshot Cicero took with his Brownie camera. Blurry—Cicero's pictures always came out blurry. In the picture they're on the porch, the four of them: Addie in her puffy dress, Bryce holding Sam in his baby blanket, Claree leaning on Bryce's arm, looking up at him, her face young and trusting.

The pain will dart into his chest. He won't be ready, but he will close his eyes anyway and force a quick prayer, *Grant me the serenity to accept the things I cannot change*, knowing as he prays that there are too many unchangeable things and not enough time to accept them all, even if he had all the time in the world.

"You bought us good shoes," Addie says. She's staring at his boots, making him glad he polished them before coming over. "You believed in good shoes."

Dear Byrd,

I wish you could know my mother, your grandmother.

When my father died, she insisted on being the one to prepare his body for the viewing. She didn't think he would trust anyone else. I took her to the funeral home, to a little room in the basement that reeked of formaldehyde despite exhaust fans that roared so hard they made our teeth chatter. My father was laid out on a table in the suit she'd chosen, his charcoal double-breasted, with a gray shirt and pink necktie. His mouth was set in a mostly straight line except for the very corner, which turned up in what looked like the beginning of a smile, like he'd just remembered a joke. My mother took off his glasses, polished them and put them back on. She smoothed makeup over the pink blotches on his face. She combed Grecian Formula into his hair and dabbed cologne behind his ears—Old Spice from the set I'd given him for his birthday. Then she stood back.

"He looks nice, doesn't he?" she said. "Dignified."

I tried to see what she saw, another version of my father—young, handsome, hopeful.

My mother came over and slipped her arm around my waist. Her arm weighed nothing. "You know," she said, "he wanted to be different. We both did."

Now that she is alone I try to visit as often as I can. She still lives in the house I grew up in, though she's made some changes. New vinyl siding—she wanted something she could clean with a garden hose. A new azalea garden with red and pink bushes given to her when my father died. She has taken down the sweet gum tree that used to shade the driveway, the tree my brother once crashed into on his silver Huffy, his first ten-speed. I remember how he came flying down the hill on School Street, turned too wide, jumped the curb, hit the tree, and was thrown into the yard. I remember the whump *when he landed. He didn't know anyone at first; he didn't recognize anything except his bike. He asked if it was damaged. I remember he said "damaged" because it sounded wrong, too old for a nine-year-old boy with blood and dirt in his mouth.*

On the sweet gum stump there's now a cast-iron cauldron brimming over with petunias, my mother's latest touch. She is redecorating her life—new flowers, new sunshine, clean new siding. Her kitchen cabinets are freshly painted; the room is brighter now. She insists on cooking when I visit and never lets me take her out. She never stops being the mother. She always pays for my gas. As soon as I arrived today, she wrote me a check for twenty dollars. You should see her penmanship. She makes her letters exactly as she was taught. Her checks are too beautiful to cash. I carry them around until she calls me complaining that she can't balance her checkbook.

We sat at the table in our regular places and held hands for grace. "We're grateful for so much food," she said. "Too much for just the two of us." She asked God to bless everyone who wasn't there—my brother and his wife, my father.

Silently I included you.

We had chicken pie and fresh summer vegetables and Sara Lee coconut cake for dessert. Then—always my favorite part—we cleared the table and washed dishes together, standing shoulder to shoulder at the sink, not talking, as if we already knew everything the other might say. My mother hummed "The Impossible Dream" in her crackly alto.

At the end of the song, she asked me, as if this somehow followed, "Didn't you go to school with the chiropractor's son?"

I almost gasped. She was asking about your father, though she doesn't know he's your father. She doesn't know there's a you. I've kept this part of my life a secret. But I have long suspected my mother of a kind of clairvoyance. An innocent, oblivious kind. She knows things she isn't aware of knowing.

"We were friends," I said.

"My friend Mary does his mother's hair. It's a shame about his little boy."

"What little boy?" Can you imagine what was going through my mind?

"Something's wrong with him, Mary says. He can't talk. The family's spent all kinds of money on doctors. He can make sounds, Mary says, but not words."

"What little boy?"

"He has a funny name," she said, frowning, trying to remember. "Smoky? Dirty?" She passed me a soapy bowl. It slipped out of my hands and crashed in the sink.

My mother gathered the shards. "You're tired," she said. "Go lie down on the couch. Take a little nap. I'll finish these."

Somehow, in all the years of trying to get on with my life—almost six years now—I never once imagined your father starting a family with anyone else. Being a father to some other son.

I especially never imagined that I would hear about it from my mother.

As I was leaving, she stood on her front porch to wave good-bye as she always does. She waved me into my car; she waved as I backed down the driveway and kept waving as I rounded the corner on School Street. I waved back. We waved and waved until we could no longer see each other.

Then I drove home and wrote you this letter.

Dear Byrd, your father has a family and it isn't us.

Key of the Angels

Dusty's birthday. He is five fingers, his whole hand.

As soon as his mother wakes up he can open his present. His mother's name is Elle: it sounds like the letter and looks the same forward and backward. She is sleeping in because it's Saturday and on Saturday his father gets up with him. His mother works in a restaurant. She works late waiting tables. She waits for people to decide what they want to eat and drink. He and his father wait for her to wake up.

"More Cheerios, buddy?" His father calls him buddy but his name is Dusty, short for Dustin, which his mother picked out. Dusty Rhodes.

He's tired of cereal. What he wants is a taste of his father's beer. He leans across his father's belly and grabs. His father's hand is long. It wraps all the way around his beer. His father says it's good to have long hands if you play guitar, which he used to do, and sometimes still does, but only for Dusty.

"Okay," his father says. "Just a sip."

They are watching his favorite video, *Home Alone*. The burglars are trying to get into the boy's house but they keep slipping on the ice. Dusty has never seen ice on sidewalks, only in drinks.

"Want to wake your mother up?" his father says.

Dusty shrugs. Sometimes his mother gets mad when they wake her up.

"Not talking today, buddy? Taking the day off?"

Some days are talking days and some aren't, it depends on how he's feeling. He likes words, he likes thinking about them, but not saying them out loud. When he tries to talk, the words get stuck in his mouth and he has to roar to make them come out. His mother once took him to a doctor who showed him how to move his mouth in different ways. At the end, the doctor said, "He's fine. He just needs practice. More conversation, less TV." His mother said thank you very fast and pushed Dusty out the door and took him for ice cream.

"REH RAYER UH," he says to his father. Let's wake her up.

"I think you just did," his father says.

Elle is pretending to sleep. Under the bed is an expensive present Roland picked out without her. She can hear them in the next room watching Dusty's *Home Alone* video with that awful little blond boy Dusty loves. Dusty is making his sounds. A good day, a talking day—it means he feels safe. She imagines him nestled on the sofa next to Roland, the warm, lumpy weight of him. She rolls onto her side and pulls up the sheet. She would like to wrap herself in their voices. She would like to stay in bed forever, feeling like a family.

The sun heats up the room. This is the nicest place Elle has lived since she came to California, a clean, carpeted two-bedroom in a big complex far away from Venice Beach, away from crowds and traffic and the constant gushing of the ocean. Away from that dingy little apartment Roland made her move out of while his North Carolina girlfriend was visiting and Elle was pretending not to mind.

It wasn't long before he asked her to move back in.

Not long after that, she got pregnant.

"I thought we were being careful," Roland said.

Elle said, "The pill isn't foolproof. It only works ninety-seven percent of the time." She didn't lie, she just left out the truth.

They got married and moved into the new apartment, which she picked out herself.

"Everything's tan," Roland said.

"Caramel," she said.

Roland got a new construction job closer to home. He played out as much as he could, while she waited tables and waited for him to *make it*—that was how he talked—or get a steady gig at least. Then the baby came and he quit, gave up his music altogether so he could spend his nights with Dusty.

"Why pay somebody?" he said.

She said, "Are you sure this is what you want?"

Pete and Golita argued with him. "Rocker to Sheetrocker," Pete said.

Roland didn't care. Just like he didn't care that he and Elle hardly ever saw each other.

She gets up and pulls the sheet off the bed. No need to keep Dusty waiting. She slides his present out from under the bed, throws the sheet over it, and carries it into the living room.

On *Home Alone*, the robbers have caught the boy and hung him on a coat rack. Dusty curls up against his father.

"Don't worry," his father says, petting him. "The old man'll save him."

Just then his mother comes out of the bedroom. She is carrying something big under a sheet.

"Happy birthday," she says.

She is standing in front of the TV; he can't see the movie. She is wearing her dotted pajamas. Her hair stands up on her head. She has spiky brown hair with yellow tips. Her eyes are bright blue like the deep end of the swimming pool. Sometimes when she looks at you it's like she's pulling you under; you want her to stop.

"Don't you want to know what it is?" she says, holding his present out in front of her.

He's afraid he won't like it. How special can it be, wrapped in a plain white sheet like she was in a hurry?

"Go on, buddy," his father says, and pauses the movie. "You've waited all morning."

Under the sheet is a black case with latches, and inside, his very own guitar, black and brown and small enough for him to hold by himself.

"A travel guitar," his father says. "You can take it with you on the road."

"It's from both of us," his mother says.

"HE YOU," Dusty says.

"You're welcome, buddy." His father tunes the guitar, then sets it across Dusty's lap and shows him where to put his hands. "Hold this string down," his father says, mashing his pointer finger, "and use this hand to strum. Like this, just these four strings. That's a G chord. Key of the angels."

Dusty practices. Playing guitar is easier than talking and sounds better.

His father goes to the closet for his own guitar. "Okay, buddy. Ready to rock?"

His father starts playing. His hand moves up and down the long part of his guitar. He makes a lot of notes. Then he nods at Dusty, and Dusty bangs out his chord.

"That's it," his father says.

His father plays more notes and Dusty hits his chord again. His father is happy. "We rock," his father says.

"REE RAH," Dusty says.

His mother is dancing in her dotted pajamas. "I'll sing," she says. "I'll be your chick singer."

"This song doesn't have words," his father says.

milestone

For the last hour she has been sitting in her front window hold-ing her phone and a Rolodex card.

Dear Byrd, there are so many questions I'm afraid to ask.

She dials Janet's number, hangs up. Dials again, hangs up.

Have no right to ask.

She dials again, this time waiting for Janet to answer. "Can you tell me how my son is doing?"

"Hold on," Janet says. There's a scrape of metal on metal as she opens her file cabinet. "I've got a letter here, his milestone letter from six years ago. You'll need to sign for it."

"I'll be right over," Addie says.

"Take your time," Janet says, without a trace of irony.

Janet hasn't changed. She looks as tired as ever. Even her dress looks the same—wrinkled, like the dress she wore to the hospital the day Byrd was born. Maybe the same dress, Addie thinks.

"Here you go." Janet hands her a plain white envelope. No

address, no postmark. Tucked inside is a letter from 1990. "It's something we require during the first year," Janet says, "before the adoption is final. A record of the child's development, his early milestones. All non-identifying, of course."

Addie turns the envelope over in her hand, again, again. "So long ago," she says. "Why didn't you tell me when it came?"

"I'm not supposed to initiate contact, not with you, not with the adoptive parents. I thought you understood."

"This is the only letter? You don't have anything more recent?"

"This is all we require." Janet smiles her tired, patient smile. "You don't have to read it here, Addie. It's yours. You can take it."

The letter is written in forward-sloping longhand on lined notebook paper. There is no greeting.

> *He was six weeks old when he first smiled.*
> *He rolled over at four months, sat up at six, crawled at nine. Now, at eleven months, he has two teeth on bottom, one and a half on top. He finger-walks—holds your finger and waddles along beside you and makes this sound: ya ya ya ya ya ya. He loves walking. He's worn holes in his sneakers.*

Addie pictures the sneakers—blue, with big white rubber toe guards.

> *He waves bye-bye. He flails his arm and smiles.*
> *He'll imitate you sticking out your tongue, but he likes it best when you imitate him. That makes him laugh. He likes to dance, which for him is bouncing up and down at the knees and turning in circles. He likes being picked up*

*and twirled and dipped. Dipping is his favorite thing. Why
do babies like to see the world upside down?*

Addie pictures them dancing in a kitchen where everything
is bright and clean and the cabinets have fresh baby latches and
the radio plays world music. The mother is barefoot, with wavy
hair and a bright, full skirt. She scoops him up in her arms, her
baby, and cha-cha-chas him across the floor. She dips him. He
squeals at the upside-down refrigerator. He is happy. He knows
she won't drop him.

The letter has no signature, only this postscript at the
bottom:

His first word was "da-da," then "ma-ma," then "bug."

Addie wonders: a fly thumping the kitchen window? An ant
in the sugar bowl? Or maybe not a bug at all, but something
that reminded him of a bug. A raisin squashed in his tiny fist.

And what about now, she wants to ask the mother. What
words does he know now?

Second Chance

John Dunn starts asking Addie what her plans are. Not in an unkind way—he would never be unkind—but in a her-own-best-interest way, which is almost worse. She figures he's tired of being sympathetic, tired of being the one to help her carry her secret around, that heavy, sloshy bucket.

Also, there's now a woman in the picture, an English professor who dresses only in black. She comes in the shop every night and leaves with John Dunn at closing. The two of them have been talking about the future.

Addie remembers thinking about the future. She remembers long-ago afternoons, sitting in Shelia's kitchen, the air warm and greasy. They played Crazy Eights and daydreamed what their lives would be. Addie never had a clear picture, only that hers would be extraordinary somehow.

"Have you ever considered opening your own store?" John Dunn asks.

The thought has crossed her mind. She has insurance money from Bryce and no one to spend it on.

"I know of a place for sale," John Dunn says. "It's in Raleigh. Second Chance, it's called. Sounds like fate, right?"

"Sounds like a pet shelter," Addie says.

But she buys the store. Fate is nothing if not heavy-handed.

Second Chance is in a two-story brick building downtown, plain except for the mural on the side from when it was a hardware store years ago. The paint is flaking off, but you can still make out the giant red hammer, cocked at an angle as if it could come smashing down any minute.

The store still smells like lime, sawdust, insecticide. Even now, customers come in from time to time looking for household items, usually old women whose husbands used to shop here. They are surprised by the books.

The manager, Peale, dresses the part, in overalls and a stiff white T-shirt and orange work boots. Like everything else, he came with the place. He is tall and thin, with skin dark as walnut, a deep part incised in his fro. He keeps a pencil tucked behind one ear and red-rimmed reading glasses on a cord around his neck. His smile is quick, bright, self-assured, genuine.

This morning he's at the front counter rummaging through a carton of books. He unearths a hardback with a purple dust jacket and holds it up to show Addie. "This poet wrote a whole book about not having children," he says. "I thought poets were supposed to know how to sum things up."

Addie wishes she could be as opinionated about anything as Peale is about everything.

He's the one who came up with their new window display, "Women Who Write Too Much: The Books of Joyce Carol Oates," because suddenly they seemed to have at least five copies of everything she had published.

Addie has been trying in small ways to make the store hers. She replaced the thick clanking cowbell on the front door with a small cast-iron garden bell that goes ca-chink ca-chink. She made a reading area for customers, with a plump sofa and an antique floor lamp and a red armchair. She has other ideas, too: Persian carpets, when she can afford them; glass-front barrister cases; a new name, when she can come up with the right one.

On the second floor—a vast, open storage area with brick walls and casement windows and oily plank floors that groan—she has carved out a small corner apartment. When she's lying in bed she can hear pigeons gurgling in the eaves, and mice thumping around, making nests in old boxes of wing nuts and washers—things that came with the store that she has no idea what to do with.

Peale leafs through the childless poet's book. "Where to shelve this? 'Fictional memoir,' it says. 'Truer than true.'"

"Memoir, I guess."

"We're out of room in memoir. Besides, if we call it memoir, people will think it's true. The regular kind of true, with facts." He slaps the book shut. "Fiction."

"I don't know," Addie says. "People will think there's a plot."

She is having coffee on the bench out front, in the shade of the awning. Across the street, a beggar takes up his post by the hotdog stand. He's there every day in his feed cap and grimy T-shirt, rattling his soup can, singing his song. *Wanna get me a hot dog, uh-huh* (clank clank clank), *quarter short.* The sycamore tree in the background is full of crows—Addie saw them fly in but she can't see them now; they're hiding in the fat leaves. She imagines them hunched together, spying on the beggar, waiting for him to spill one of his coins.

This is her favorite time of day: Hillsborough Street waking up. Down the block, three girls sleepwalk into the coffee shop. A couple comes out buzzing. A woman in high-heeled sandals trip-trops down the sidewalk, chattering into a cell phone. A man in an SUV rolls up to the traffic light and lowers his window. He is bald, with a pink bullet-shaped head—probably he shaves it so that people will think going bald was his idea. "Hey, sweet thang," he calls, and the cell phone woman looks up, but she isn't the one he means. He's calling at a cop reading meters.

The cop calls back, "Why don't you get your hair cut?"

An ordinary day. An ordinary life. Exactly what she never thought she wanted.

Lullaby

Dusty's mom talks while she drives. She says, "You can't let your heart stay broken your whole life." She says, "You have to know when to cut your losses."

They are on a long highway, driving with the windows rolled down because there's no air conditioning and it's night and his mom says he should try and go to sleep but he never sleeps in the car. He likes to look at things. Besides, how can he sleep when she keeps talking?

"When to hold and when to fold," she says. Her hair is sweaty and flat, the little spikes all wilted. The tattoo on her neck looks like a polka dot. A ladybird, she calls it.

What Dusty wants to know is when his dad will catch up with them. Already they are far from home.

"When to walk, when to run." His mom is singing, sort of.

They are on a long highway and she is driving fast with her eyes straight ahead, not looking at him. Sometimes they stop and buy Cokes and M&Ms out of machines. They go to the bathroom and she brings out wet paper towels and they dab their faces. This is the hottest night that has ever been. His mom drives fast, trying to cool them off, but the air coming in the windows is hot and smells bad. At one place the smell is so bad he has to throw up, but his mom says this does not make him a baby. She says the smell is cows being killed and from now on they will never eat another hamburger. "When we get to Reno, we'll be vegetarians," she says. "You and me."

Sometimes the highway is dark, sometimes it's lit up by cars, sometimes by big colored signs. He likes the signs that flash. He hopes his mom will change her mind about driving all night and stop at one of the flashing motels. He hopes it will have a swimming pool, and his dad will come, and they'll all go for a swim, and afterwards his dad will take them out for pancakes even though it's still dark outside, and his mom and dad will be glad to see each other, and they'll let him have extra syrup.

Elle is exhausted. She sinks onto the edge of her bed and the chenille spread slides around underneath her. Dusty is asleep in the other bed. His face is not peaceful like a child's but tired like a man's.

Her aunt's guest room—her old room—has green wallpaper with tiny white flowers, baby's breath. Baby's breath is for remembering. She wishes she could remember something about Roland that would make her time with him not seem like a waste. Anything, just one small memory to rub around in her mind and put a shine on, like a lucky penny.

She has to go back eight years, before Dusty, to when Roland called her and said, "You want to try again? I miss you." The way he said "miss," it sounded like love. He came for her in his van and loaded her things and moved her back into his apartment, and she walked in expecting to be relieved and happy, expecting the place to look different somehow, but it was just as dingy and sad as before. Only one thing had changed: he had emptied out a drawer in his bureau to make room for the clothes and things she'd always kept in a box. He had made a space for her.

That can be her penny. His empty drawer.

Dusty, pretending to sleep, watches her through his eyelashes. She's sitting on her bed with her head in her hands. Her hair is brown with yellow tips and her hands are in it like she's feeling around for something, and she's rocking back and forth, back and forth, making a little sound with her throat. Her bedspread is slipping, but she keeps rocking, and he's getting tired but he can't fall asleep because then who would watch her, who would hear her sing?

Red Hammer

Sometimes it takes a new person to call you by your true name.

William Glass, Peale's friend, is a mural artist. He wants Addie to hire him to restore the big flaking-off hammer on the side of her store. Addie wonders if they shouldn't have a new image, something to do with books. "No," William says. "Absolutely not. This place *is* the red hammer."

And there it is, the name she's been casting around for, so obvious it never occurred to her: Red Hammer Books.

Peale approves, even if it wasn't his idea.

"You don't think it sounds too hardware-store?" Addie says. She has rejected all of Peale's names—Buddenbooks, Wrinkly Reader, Tome Main, Dustjacket Sins.

"We *are* a hardware store," Peale says. "We're the hardware store of used bookstores." He tells a story about a man who recently called asking for a book he'd seen in new arrivals. The man couldn't remember the title or the author, only that the book had a green cover. Dusty green, like a chalkboard.

"Fiction or nonfiction?" Peale had asked.

The man didn't know. He didn't want the book to read, he wanted it for the cover. He wanted to paint his house that shade of green.

"Book green," William says.

"*Used*-book green," Peale says.

William's hands are knobby, his fingernails outlined with paint. He smells faintly of solvent. He is tall, but bows his head like he's trying to reduce the distance between him and everyone else. Broad-shouldered, with silver-brown hair. Handsome in an arty, unkempt way. He and Peale look to Addie like older versions of the *Mod Squad* guys.

"If I dye my hair blond," she says, "can I be Julie?"

It isn't just a matter of dabbing paint in blank spots. William takes photographs. He makes sketches. He scrapes off loose paint. He draws outlines in chalk so that he can erase his mistakes with wet rags.

The street people are curious. Every morning they come pecking around him like pigeons. He hires them to sweep up paint chips, hand his rags up and down, move his ladder. He pays them with footlongs and pink lemonades from Snoopy's.

When it rains, the street people huddle under the stairwell at Cooper Square to keep dry; William comes into the store. He leans on the counter and rifles though just-arrived books. He likes to collect things he finds in them—receipts, business cards, pressed flowers. He collects inscriptions, copying them into the blue spiral notebook he carries around everywhere.

He shows Addie this one from *Sister to Sister: Women Write about the Unbreakable Bond.*

Christmas 1995. Maybe this book will help explain our friendship. Read it when you need encouragement. My sister = my best friend. I love you. Love, Leslie

What's curious, he says, is how this book ended up in a used bookstore, why Leslie's sister didn't want it.

Addie guesses maybe it embarrassed her. The pink cover, the girls in straw hats, Leslie's loopy handwriting.

"No," William says, "I think it was something else. The unbreakable bond broke."

It's less of a mystery how they ended up with *The Audubon Guide to Fishes and Mammals*, inscribed, "To Michael, who thinks and acts and smells like a fish. Happy birthday, your dad."

A State student brings in a stack of Viking Classic paperbacks, including a copy of *Madame Bovary* on which someone has scrawled in thick black ink, "What should Emma do? Change her expectations!"

Addie says, "Sorry, we don't buy books with the answers on the cover."

It's an actual policy, one they had to make after Vivian, a part-time clerk who also came with the store, bought a box of Agatha Christies from a customer who had written the name of the murderer on every title page.

"How could you not have noticed?" Addie asked her.

"Well," Vivian said, "you still have to read the book to find out if the answer's right."

William says his favorite writer in high school was J.D. Salinger. "I felt like I was related to the Glass family," he confides to Addie. "Their long-lost brother William. For a while I even tried to write like Buddy Glass."

"Lots of words?"

"And parentheses."

"Footnotes."

"Italics, *lots* of italics." William smiles. He has brown eyes, hopeful, hungry, trusting. Like the eyes of a dog, Addie thinks. A dog can see into you, all your secrets, and still not leave you; that's what people say. She has never had a dog.

"Now you," he says. "Tell me an embarrassing secret."

"But that wasn't embarrassing," Addie says. "Salinger was *every*body's favorite."

"Not everybody pretended to be a Salinger character."

"Yes, they did."

"Tell me a secret anyway."

"Okay. Here's something I've never told anybody. I've never understood all the fuss over *Madame Bovary*."

William laughs—a furry, barking laugh.

He always shows up when he says he's going to. He always tells Addie what he's doing so she'll know what she's paying him for. Once the basic mural is done, he says, he's going to "ghost" it—sand it with a belt sander, apply milk wash, tea stain. Spatter white paint to make bird poop. "It'll look like it's been here forever," he says.

He talks to Addie about her work. "Bookseller—a perfect word. Double o's, double l's, k in the middle, breaking things up. Like a bookend in the middle of a shelf."

He makes it seem okay to love your work and not worry about other things you would rather love.

On story mornings, another Peale idea, children line up on the sofa like dolls. Boys swing their legs, girls tug at their hair bows while their mothers browse the store for books they will never have time to read.

One week Peale invites William to lead story morning.

"William here is a mural painter," Peale announces to the children. "Any of you know what that is?"

The children stare mutely at William. His face is clean-shaven and bright, his hair still damp from the shower. He's wearing a clean black T-shirt and clean black jeans. He says, "Who's heard of Roy Lichtenstein? Diego Rivera? Famous mural painters. My heroes." He holds up a book he found on the art shelf. "This is one of Diego's murals. He was Mexican. Who knows where Mexico is? Diego used to eat people. He liked women best, their legs and brains."

"Ew," a boy says.

"Ew," another boy says.

A girl in pink raises her hand. "I don't think that's true," she says. "I think you made that up."

"Be polite," Peale says, and smiles at the girl so hard he scares her.

"What murals did you paint?" asks the boy sitting next to her. He is fat, with rolls in his neck and arms.

"I'm repainting the red hammer on the side of this store, for one," William says.

"What else?"

"Have you seen the new restaurant in City Market, across from where they drop the big nut at New Year's? I painted that mural."

"It's an acorn," the girl says. "The nut is an acorn."

"Correct," William says. "You, young lady, know your nuts."

"Read to us," she says.

William takes out his blue spiral notebook. He runs his hand through his hair. "Want to hear a story I wrote?"

"Yeah!" the boys yell.

"Okay, but remember, I'm a painter, not a writer. I just sometimes write things down. This is called 'People in Cars.'"

He begins: "One day, everybody in cars forgot where they were going. A lot of them went to work because they couldn't think what else to do. Some made U-turns and headed back home or wherever they'd started from. Some pulled off the road and parked. Some took naps. They hoped everything would be fine when they woke up, but even in their dreams they were lost."

One boy looks worried. He kicks at the sofa.

"Some just kept driving. They thought if they drove long enough they would get to the right place, wherever that was. Unless they ran out of gas first. They couldn't ask for directions, because what would they have said? 'Excuse me, where am I going?'"

They laugh. "Excuuuuse me," the fat boy says.

"Is that story true?" the girl says.

William continues: "Nobody knew everybody else was lost. They all thought they were the only ones. They started getting mad. Pretty soon they were all yelling and flipping the bird and crashing their cars into each other."

"Flipping the bird!" the fat boy screams. He slides closer to the girl, crowding her.

She shoves him away. "Then what?" she says.

"The end," William says.

"That's not a story. Read a real story. Read Angelina Ballerina."

"Crash!" the fat boy says, and pounds the girl's arm.

The business next door, Curtain Call, sells theater curtains. Women show up for work early every morning wearing smocks and carrying Tupperware lunches. Their husbands drop them off. From her upstairs window, Addie watches the women kiss their husbands goodbye, then disappear down a hole in the sidewalk. They will spend the day in a basement full of sewing machines and bolts of flame-retardant velvet, coming up only for cigarette breaks and lunch.

Sometimes William calls to them from his ladder. Addie can hear him—"Beautiful morning, ladies"—but they never answer. They just go on smoking, eating, blinking like they've never seen the sun.

swifts

William has been watching them all summer, counting. He wants to show someone. He wants to show Addie.

He picks her up at quarter to seven. The evening is hot, thick, no breeze. His truck's air conditioner doesn't work, so he turns on the fan he keeps clipped to the dash. When Addie gets in, it blows her scent around—sweet, soft, papery, like books. She's wearing a loose dress, green like her eyes.

"Where are we going?" she says.

"You'll see."

He drives to the empty parking lot on Wilmington Street across from the Hudson Belk building. The store has been closed a long time. The windows are full of naked mannequins with vacant, dreamy faces. William parks, gets out, takes his cooler from behind his seat, opens the tailgate of the truck, and lays out a picnic supper: egg salad sandwiches, pickles, ice-cold bottles of Jamaican ginger ale. He wonders if a man has ever made Addie a picnic. He opens a bottle of ginger ale and hands it to her and she tilts her head back to drink. Her neck is long and thin. The bottle sweats.

"Mm," she says. "Spicy."

The sky is changing. Dusk is setting in.

They eat their sandwiches. "This is the best egg salad I've ever had," Addie says, "and I'm an egg salad connoisseur." Her face is luminous. She looks like nothing could ever make her happier than to be sitting on this tailgate in this parking lot eating this sandwich. William still hasn't told her what they're waiting for. She doesn't even know they're waiting.

"Kalamata olives," he says, "chopped fine. That's my secret."

At exactly seven twenty, there is a loud whirring overhead and the sky clouds over, full of shadows, tiny black zeppelins.

"What are they?" Addie says, dabbing egg salad from the corner of her mouth.

"Chimney swifts."

The birds fly in a giant storm cloud toward the Hudson Belk chimney and begin their wide circling. They look like a cyclone. For five, ten minutes, they spiral down.

William watches Addie's flickering eyes, the tiny shadows swimming across her face.

"There must be a thousand of them," she says.

"Four thousand."

"You're making that up."

He shakes his head. He doesn't want her to think he knows too much.

"How do they all fit? Where do they perch?"

"They don't perch. They don't have feet, just little hooks that clamp onto the mortar."

"What do they do in there?"

"Nothing. Sleep. They're too crowded to move. They're too close even to mate."

They sit and watch as gradually the birds disappear into the chimney. Light drains from the sky. William starts to gather up the remains of their picnic.

"Wait," Addie says. She looks sad, slightly dazed, the way William always feels when the birds are in for the night. "Is there anything you don't pay attention to?" she asks him. Then she leans over and kisses him on the cheek, a kiss so quick and light he will later wonder if it really happened.

Jackpot Land

Midnight. The sodium vapor light in the parking lot shines into Roland's living room, giving it an amber cast. Otherwise the apartment is dark. Roland is sitting on the sofa, holding the telephone in his lap, receiver pressed to one ear. He counts rings, wonders if she'll pick up. He wishes he hadn't quit smoking. He could kill for a cigarette.

Three, four. How many until her machine clicks on?

He tried her old number first, in Greensboro, but it was no longer in service. He talked to three different operators before he found a listing in Raleigh.

He's about to hang up when the ringing stops. "Addie," he says before she can speak, "guess who this is."

"Hello?" she says.

"It's me. Roland Rhodes."

"How many Rolands do you think I know?" she says.

He laughs. He can't tell if she's making a joke.

"So," he says, "how are you?"

"Asleep."

He wonders if she's alone. She sounds alone. There's no background voice asking "Who is it, what time is it?"

"What time is it?" she says.

"It's late. I'm sorry. I shouldn't have called."

"What's wrong, Roland? Is something wrong?"

"You're mad."

"I'm not mad. Tell me what's wrong."

"I'll call back when you're awake. I'm sorry, baby."

He hangs up, walks to the kitchen, pulls a Dixie cup out of the dispenser and fills it with Jack Daniels. The cup has a Donald Duck on it. Elle hung the dispenser next to the sink where Dusty could reach it. Dusty likes to pull his own cups.

It's been almost a week since they left. Roland didn't understand at first what had happened. He'd come home Monday night so Elle could hand Dusty off and go to work as usual, but she and Dusty weren't there, and there was no note. He called the restaurant. He called Elle's friends. No one had seen her. Finally, not knowing what else to do, he called the police. They patched him through to a woman officer. "My wife and son are missing," he said. "Are their clothes missing?" the policewoman asked. He had to put down the phone and go look. It embarrassed him to have to say, "Yes. She took clothes. She took the suitcases."

Two days later, Elle called. She had taken Dusty to Reno. They were staying with her aunt and uncle, she said. Her uncle was going to get her a job in a casino.

"You're in Reno," Roland said, but saying it didn't make it real.

"Yeah."

"Jackpot land."

"Don't kid yourself," she said. "This isn't about money."

"Then what?"

"It's you and me, Roll. We're just killing time."

"That's not fair," he said.

She was quiet. He could hear her breathing, waiting. He knew if he said the right thing he could change her mind.

He said, "You can't just take him."

She hung up.

He has spent a week wondering what to do. He can't go to a lawyer. No money. He can't go to his parents—who wants to deal with Pet on top of everything else? He needs somebody to help him figure things out. Somebody smart. Somebody who gets him, who'll be nice. He doesn't know many nice people.

Addie was dreaming when the phone rang, and the ringing became part of her dream. Then Roland's voice became part of the dream. It was a dream she'd had before: Roland calling, wanting something. As always, before she could wake up, he was gone.

Now she can't sleep. The traffic light outside her window is blinking amber. The light makes a sound when it blinks, a tiny wet click, the sound an eyelid would make if you could hear it opening and closing.

She picks up the phone again and presses star-sixty-nine. A machine answers. "We're sorry," the voice says, "the last number that called yours is not known. This call was received on July twenty-eighth, nineteen ninety-seven, at two fifty-four a.m. Please hang up now."

She goes to her desk and tries the Internet but finds only one Roland Rhodes, the president of a chemical company in Kansas City. There's a picture of him on his company website, a gray-haired man with a thin mustache. His company makes pesticides. He shows up on other websites, too. He's very active in the pest control community, lecturing at conferences, giving money to agricultural schools. The secretary-treasurer of United Producers, Formulators, and Distributors. Not the kind of man who would sit up late at night calling old girl-friends. Or whatever she is to her Roland Rhodes, who still uses both names with her, in case she has forgotten him.

Only Life

At forty-one, Addie is taking soy vitamins for hot flashes. She rinses her hair with henna to color the gray.

William is forty-three and wears gel inserts in his shoes.

Neither of them thinks of love the way they used to, as something to be fallen into, like a bed or a pit. It isn't big and deep and abstract. Love is particulate. It's fine. It accumulates like dust.

William sketches Addie sitting in the red chair with the sun coming in through the window Peale has just washed. She is holding a leather-bound copy of *Moby-Dick*.

"You know what Eudora Welty said about *Moby-Dick*," Peale says.

"What," they say.

"He was a symbol of so much, he had to be a whale."

On fall nights William and Addie go driving. William picks Addie up at the store after closing and they drive through State campus down Western Boulevard to Avent Ferry Road, out past the shopping centers and apartments and subdivisions, out past Lake Johnson, into the country, all the way to Holly Springs. The road through the country is narrow and rolling, lined with fences and barns. They drive past farmhouses with shades drawn, their windows yellow blanks. A few porches have jack-o'-lanterns.

William likes to imagine living in one of the houses. Coming in from his farm every evening, sitting down to supper with his family, clearing the table afterwards, helping the kids with their homework, teaching them long division, tucking them into bed. He and his wife sit up and read for a while, maybe watch a little TV. He goes to bed first. When he's almost asleep his wife comes in and lies down behind him. She laces her arms around him. He can feel her breasts against his back, her heart thumping.

Addie keeps silent on these drives. She pretends this is the only life she's ever had, in William's truck, with William driving, and all she can hear is the hum of tires on the highway, and crickets. Always crickets, even in October.

William takes her flowers on Valentine's Day, three dozen perfect red roses he has scavenged from a florist's dumpster because he knows she loves flowers but not extravagance or waste. He knows she will love rescued roses in a way she could not love paid-for roses.

Addie loves the sound of William, the quiet of him. The soft thump of his jeans dropping on the floor. His breath, which is quiet even when he's breathing hard. He doesn't talk when they have sex, or make her say what she wants. He keeps his eyes open all the way to the end. He doesn't go inside himself like other men. With other men, you could be anyone. With William she is Addie.

He falls asleep curled against her, front to front, and she rubs her hands up and down his back, like she can learn him by his skin and bones.

They are in her apartment. It's not yet dawn but she has an early appointment so she's up already, standing over her sock drawer, deciding what to wear, mumbling to herself—quietly, she thinks, but she wakes William.

"Are you praying to your socks?" he says.

He always wakes up awake. It's because he doesn't dream, he says. He doesn't have that layer to pass through.

"Sorry," she tells him. "Go back to sleep."

"You never know," he says. "God might be socks."

Addie and William like discovering important books that aren't as famous as they should be, like *The Diviners* by Margaret Laurence, and *The Brothers K* by David James Duncan. Addie starts a list, "Unheard-of Masterpieces," and posts it in the store by the cash register.

"You never know," William says. "One list in one store could change history."

William believes that no act, if it's purposeful, is too small. He protests junk mail by filling postage-paid return envelopes from one company with advertisements from another. Addie follows his example and sends *Time* magazine the fake check for $58,000 that came from the credit card company.

William lives in a house on a hill on a cut-through street where drivers often speed. He has made a sign for his front yard, a black sandwich board painted with big yellow letters, and set it perpendicular to the street so that it can be seen from both directions. One side says, THIS IS A NEIGHBOR-HOOD WITH CHILDREN. The other says, SLOW THE FUCK DOWN.

William is an open book, not afraid for people to know him. He throws big parties even though his house is gutted and full of lumber for the walls and cabinets he is going to build. On the Saturday before Easter, he has an egg-decorating party for all his artist friends. He rents folding tables and chairs. He orders dyes from a Ukrainian shop in New York. On the morning of the party he buys eggs, organic white ones that haven't been scrubbed. He spreads newspapers and sets out votive candles and tins of beeswax and tiny tools with special names, and his artist friends come and sit around the tables and make egg art. They've all done this before: they know how to draw fine lines with wax, they know to use the pale dyes before the dark. They carry their finished eggs to the kitchen and blow them out in a big metal bowl in the sink. Raw-egg smell fills the house and makes Addie nauseous. This is her first time at the party, her first time decorating eggs that aren't hardboiled, and she does things backwards, blows out her egg first so that it can't be dipped in dye, but she doesn't want to waste the perfect eggshell so she glues cotton to it and makes a face and legs out of clay and calls it a sheep. It's primitive, something a child might make. But William tells her he loves it, the wistful little face. He holds it up for his friends.

"I drank too much," Addie says on Easter Sunday. She is helping William put the egg things away. "My hands won't stop shaking. I can't remember a thing I said to your friends last night, but I remember talking. I talk too much. My father always called me a bigmouth."

"Did you know," William says, "the mouth on the Statue of Liberty is three feet wide?"

To cure her hangover he takes her out for hot fudge sundaes. It's a sunny day and the patio at Goodberry's is crowded with slouchy, flirty teenagers, parents with strollers, children pitching pennies in the fountain. Car radios blare from the parking lot.

Everyone loves ice cream, especially Addie. William is unnerved by how fast her sundae disappears.

Addie has a scar across her lower abdomen in the shape of a smile. She won't let anyone see it. When she and William have sex, she turns off the lights.

One night, in the dark, under the covers, he runs his finger across it. He is gentle and doesn't ask any questions. Addie doesn't offer any answers.

Sometimes Addie wonders who will die first, she or William. She imagines the two of them old, their faces wrinkled, their eyes sunken but alert, stealing worried glances at each other, waiting.

William is not afraid of dying. He is afraid of being left. Three women have left him so far: his mother, who died when he was thirteen; a woman he lived with, who said he needed her too much; and another woman he lived with, who said he was too self-sufficient and didn't need her enough.

Addie is afraid of her secret. Not that she gave up her child, which William would forgive, but that she didn't tell Roland. Who would stay with someone like that?

A woman comes in the store with a grocery bag full of Joni Mitchell CDs. The woman is middle-aged, wearing a dowdy sweater, but there is something young and dimly hopeful in her face, some girlish devotion. Addie pictures her as a teenager, lying across her bed, listening to music on Saturday nights when other girls were out on dates, playing her favorite songs again and again, memorizing the lyrics. Collecting every Joni Mitchell album. Eventually replacing the albums with CDs. Buying every new release, though she liked the music less and less, believing that sooner or later she'd be rewarded, sooner or later there would be another *Blue*, another *Court and Spark*, another *Hissing of Summer Lawns* or *Hejira*. Now, finally, after so many years, she's come to understand: there will be no going back, for her or for Joni. You'd think this would make her even more grateful for Joni's old music, but no, just the opposite. Now she can't listen to Joni at all without feeling betrayed.

Addie sees this a lot in the store: devoted readers turning on their favorite writers when the writers run out of things to say or interesting ways to say them.

The woman sets her bag on the counter and in a high, round voice that sounds a little Canadian, a little like Joni, asks Peale what he will give her for "the complete discography."

"We don't buy music," he says.

The woman has the grace of someone used to disappointment. "Thanks anyway," she says, and carries her bag out of the store as hopefully as she entered. The front door ca-chinks behind her. Addie watches her down the sidewalk, her slow, careful stride, the way she cradles her bag in both arms.

That night with William, Addie puts on *Blue* and they listen to Joni sing about all the people she ever lost or hurt. Joni's voice is young and pure and sad. She is famous for her sadness.

Before she got famous, everyone now knows, Joni had a baby daughter and gave her up. Recently the daughter found Joni. Their reunion was in the news. Almost every news story mentioned the "clues" Joni had left for the daughter in her music, though really there was just the one song, "Little Green"—never one of Addie's favorites—and a couple of lines in another. It didn't matter anyway, because the daughter grew up never hearing any of Joni's music except for the duet she did with Seal.

Addie has seen pictures of the daughter. She is beautiful, with long blond hair and high cheekbones. She is even more beautiful than Joni. When she and Joni were first reunited, she was gracious. She told reporters she was proud of her mother for making something of her life. Then Joni left her again to go on tour, and the daughter fell apart. She fought with Joni. Their fights were in the news. Addie tried to imagine them: the daughter saying to Joni, *Tell me again why you gave me up.* Joni saying, *I had a gift. I had a responsibility to my gift. And besides, why would you want to be raised by someone who wasn't cut out to be a mother?*

"What?" William says. He is holding Addie's feet in his lap, moving them to the music.

"Nothing."

I'm not like Joni, she thinks. *I didn't trade my child for a music career. I gave him up for nothing.*

Sometimes she and William hold hands, which makes Addie feel very young or very old instead of middle-aged. The best place for holding hands is the movie theater, where it's dark and intimate and you can sit for a long time.

They are regulars at the Rialto. They go see whatever is playing there. The current movie is *Sliding Doors*, with Gwyneth Paltrow. This is Addie's favorite kind of movie, a what-if, where the main character gets a chance to see how her life might have turned out if fate hadn't stepped in, if she hadn't missed her train, hit her head, dropped her earring. If she'd chosen someone else. If she'd wanted a family.

Reno

Nevada is hot, brown, and poisonous, full of rattlesnakes, black widows, scorpions, casinos, whorehouses, nuclear dumps. Water is scarce. People eat their meals off buffets, get brain cancer, have run-ins with aliens, gamble themselves bankrupt. Nevada is the suicide capital of the country. Every summer, at a festival in the desert north of Reno, a big wooden effigy is set on fire and everybody chants *Burn the man*. The cities sound like slot machines. Nobody sleeps.

Frank Zappa once said, "You can't always write a chord ugly enough to say what you want to say."

But for Elle, Nevada is home. And home, or the memory of home, still has a kind of magic. As a young child, she lived with her parents in Reno, in a bungalow with a view of the Truckee River. Every morning her mother would open the curtains and the sun would flash on the river and the ground would come alive with robins and quail. Evenings, if her father got home from work in time, he would take her to Virginia Street to watch the arch light up.

In 1972, when she was not yet twelve years old, her parents were killed in a car crash. It happened on a Saturday in spring. Her parents were on their way home from Pyramid Lake, where they'd been fishing since dawn. They were driving the new Ford Pinto, shiny and brown as a bean. Elle wasn't with them; she had slept over with her cousins, who lived in a brick house with shag carpet and a console color TV. It was lunchtime. Elle and her cousins were spread out on the living room floor eating pizza and watching *Soul Train* when, twenty-five miles north of town, the Pinto swerved off the highway. Elle's father overcorrected, the car flipped, and the gas tank exploded. There were no other cars around, no witnesses, no evidence except tire marks and smoldering remains. The trooper who came to notify the family—a short man with a thick, embarrassed neck—couldn't say absolutely that Elle's parents had been killed on impact, but thought it likely, based on his experience. He didn't know what caused the Pinto to swerve. Elle imagined a gust of wind, or an animal darting in front of the car, a rabbit or dog or coyote. Or maybe it was the shadow of a bird flying over. In the desert, shadows can play tricks.

Elle's aunt and uncle, who had two sons and a daughter of their own, took her in, and Elle shared a room with her girl cousin. She never stopped missing her parents or feeling the awful mix of guilt and relief that she hadn't gone with them. But her aunt and uncle were determined to make her happy, or less unhappy. They took her places, bought her things: clothes, makeup, records, posters for her wall. Her cousins treated her like a sister.

In spite of everyone's kindness, or maybe because of it, Elle left Reno as soon as she was old enough to claim her small inheritance. She moved to L.A.—for good, she thought—telling her aunt and uncle she wanted to be in a place with an ocean.

In fact what she wanted was a place where people wouldn't feel the need to be kind.

Nineteen years later, she's back, sharing her old room with Dusty until her aunt can redecorate the boys' room. Everything is the same as before: twin beds, chenille spreads, flowery wallpaper. "Gus roo," Dusty calls it. *Girls' room.*

Elle's uncle gets her a job as a cocktail waitress in a casino on Virginia Street. She is thirty-seven, old for cocktailing, and jobs aren't as plentiful since the Indian casinos began cutting into Reno's business, but Elle's uncle has connections.

"See?" Elle says to Dusty. "Our luck is changing."

She works the graveyard shift. Her aunt drives Dusty to and from school every day and takes care of him afternoons while Elle sleeps. Dusty goes to public school where he meets with a speech therapist but is otherwise in a regular class since he can read and write as well as anybody in second grade—better, in fact, because of his speech problem. When he writes, people understand him. He carries a memo pad in his pocket at all times.

Every evening at six, Elle gets out of bed and cooks supper—pancakes or eggs if she's in a breakfast mood, otherwise macaroni and cheese, Boca burgers, tofu dogs. She's making vegetarians of them all. Her aunt and uncle like their steaks and chops, but they are gracious and accept Elle's cooking as her contribution to the household.

Most nights after supper, Roland calls from California. He talks to Dusty first, then to Elle. "What's in Reno that isn't here?" he asks her. "What do you want?"

"I want to be somebody," she says, quietly, so no one in the house can hear her.

"You are," he says.

"Somebody important," she says.

"You are," he says. "You're my wife."

"More important than that."

"You're the mother of my son."

"More important than that."

In the casino where she works there's no night or day, only flashing lights and gaudy chandeliers and mirrored ceilings and patterned carpets that reek of cigarette smoke and fried food. Elle wears a strapless uniform and black stockings and serves drinks to people in vacation clothes. The losers are sad, but the winners are worse: men with chips piled in front of them, loud men with gold chains and ruddy faces, their eyes narrow and black as seeds. She bends over when she serves them and they give her big tips.

When her shift is over she puts on sunglasses and walks outside. The morning light is painful. The younger waitresses like to put off daylight for another hour or two by going to the casino across the street. It's their way of being friendly without having to get to know each other.

One morning they invite Elle to go with them. They don't know her. They don't know she's just left her husband. They don't even know she has a husband, or a son.

"Okay," she says, trying not to sound excited.

She hasn't gambled since she was a child learning poker from her uncle. He taught her Texas Hold 'Em, Omaha Hi-Lo, Four-and-Four, Lamebrains, Criss-Cross, Night Baseball, and Follow the Queen—Elle's favorite, a seven-card stud game in which the card that follows a turned-up queen is wild, and whenever another queen is turned up, the wild card changes. Elle and her uncle and cousins would sit around the kitchen table wearing visored caps, eating sliced bologna on saltines with mustard. Her uncle had names for the cards: Fever, Sexy, Savannah, Eddie, Arnold, Typewriter, Jake, Pretty Lady, Cowboy. He was not a sentimental teacher; he never purposely let anyone win, and Elle rarely did. Even playing penny-ante she sometimes lost all her allowance money. "I told you not to bluff," her uncle would say. "In a low-stakes game it doesn't pay to bluff because you can't force anybody out. In a wild card game, don't bet without a wild card."

The casino across the street is bigger than the one where she works, with more machines and more tables. She's intimidated by table poker, and she doesn't want to throw her money away on the slots like the other waitresses. Just inside the door there's a bank of video poker machines. She sits down at the first open one, an old machine with ghosts of cards burned into the screen. She slides in a twenty, the only cash she has. The game is Jacks or Better.

After ten minutes she's lost most of her money. She knows her uncle would tell her to stop while she still has enough for a pack of cigarettes. What keeps her playing isn't a feeling of luck, but something more dangerous: the feeling of having nothing to lose.

She presses a button and the machine deals her two spades, the nine and ten, and three diamonds, the jack, queen, and king—a straight. She can feel her life changing. A man walks up beside her. He is thin and sallow, with combed-back hair. His eyes are hard; he isn't smiling. "Go for it," he says, his voice low and serious. Elle thinks he must know something. She decides to draw to her diamonds. And sure enough, the miracle that will ruin her: the ten and ace appear. A buzzer goes off. People in the casino look up. The other waitresses, her new friends, leave their machines and come over. "What nerve," they say, "to go for the royal!" She beams and clutches her pay ticket. Her heart is beating all the way into her fingertips.

She looks around for her mystery man, but he is lost in the crowd, so completely gone she wonders if he was ever there at all.

Dusty never talks at the supper table. He doodles in his memo pad and waits for his father to call.

One night Elle has had enough. "I asked you not to do that," she says, and snatches the pad away. The pages are covered with drawings of guitars, cutaways like Roland's. The drawings are tiny and perfect and make Elle even angrier.

She changes her strategy, increases her bets. She stays out later every morning. Some days she doesn't get home until noon, and by then she is almost too tired to sleep. She closes the thick rubber shades that make her room look like night. She turns on a floor fan to filter out noise. The fan sounds like an ocean. It makes her think of California, and of Roland. During her first year with him, they went through her inheritance. She wonders if it's possible to win back everything she has lost.

A week after Dusty's eighth birthday, a package arrives in the mail: Roland's old jean jacket. Dusty loves it. Elle has never seen him love anything so much. He insists on wearing it every day, even in the heat. It swallows him, makes him look small and lost.

A royal should come up on average about once every forty thousand hands, so sooner or later she's bound to hit another one. The key is speed. The faster she plays, the sooner she'll win. So far she has used up her initial winnings and is down a thousand, but she isn't discouraged. She doesn't think of losing as losing, she thinks of it as investing, preparing to win again.

She always plays the same machine. It's comfortable, the seat far enough from the screen that she can see all the cards without moving her head. She uses both hands on the deal and hold buttons. She builds up credits so that she isn't constantly pumping in money.

If she doesn't stop to eat or smoke, she can play six hundred games an hour.

Roland says he wants to be a family again. He's moving to Reno. Elle has to remind herself that this is what she's been waiting for.

Her uncle rents them an apartment. He wants to help them the way Roland's parents helped them in California, when they were first taking Dusty to doctors.

The apartment is half of a duplex, a small, flat building on a street of small flat buildings with chain-link fences and skinny, creaking cottonwood trees and dogs that bare their teeth when they bark. Each side of the duplex has its own garage. Elle and Roland have never had a garage. It's small and dark like their apartment, and airless, barely wide enough for a single car, but it has an automatic door and automatic lights.

Their one bit of affluence.

Elle's uncle sets Roland up in a training course for slot technicians. He says it's important for a man to feel like he can support his family, and slot techs make good money. Roland says to Elle, "I'm too old to be going back to school." He's forty-two. In the time they've been apart, not quite a year, he's begun to go bald like his father. Elle doesn't mind. It's a relief to know that from now on, she will look better than him. He can be the one who worries.

"You're not old," she says. "You're middle-aged."

He takes classes called Introduction to Slots, Money Validation, Applications of Electricity, Slot Mechanics, Slot Electronics, Slot Microprocessors, and Troubleshooting. After six months, he gets a certificate. Elle frames it for him. She is trying to be happy.

One night while she's in the bedroom getting dressed for work, Roland walks up behind her and wraps his arms around her waist. They look at each other in the mirror. "You look good," he tells her. Her skin is smooth and clear. Her hair is a single color now—a blond so pale it looks ivory, like a wedding gown—and she's let it grow longer and she uses a lotion that makes it curly.

"I do what I can," she says.

"You know," he says, "things are going to be different this time."

She pets his arm. She wants to believe him. But besides having him back, and living in the duplex, not much has changed. She still spends her nights cocktailing, her mornings at her machine, her afternoons sleeping. Her aunt keeps Dusty after school and Roland picks him up in the evening. When they come home, Elle gets out of bed and cooks supper and they eat at the coffee table so that Roland can watch *Wonder Years* reruns on TV, the show that opens with Joe Cocker singing "With a Little Help from my Friends."

"Those were my years," Roland tells Dusty.

She slides her hands up and down the sides of her machine, where the brass plating has worn off. She closes her eyes and pictures her mystery man with his slicked-back hair. "Talk to me," she says. "Talk to me."

The wind in Nevada is full of grit. Gold dust, Roland calls it.

He lands a day job at a casino in Sparks. Every night he comes home with the casino smell—smoke, grease, stale cologne. Elle has it too, though she never knew until she smelled it on Roland. Sometimes when they lie in bed together she can't tell his skin from hers.

The duplex is small and looks dirty even when it's clean. The sink clogs, the toilet backs up. Things break. One morning while Roland is showering, the nozzle flies off and hits him on the head.

They talk about saving for a house. They're both making decent money. Roland is over his cocaine habit—he quit cold turkey soon after Elle and Dusty left him—and he's been turning over his paycheck so that he can't ruin their finances again. He has turned everything over to Elle so that whatever happens this time can't be his fault.

Every day on her way home, Elle stops in the post office and collects the mail—bills, advertisements, bank statements. She knows how close to broke they are, but she doesn't tell Roland. She doesn't want him to know how much she's investing in her machine.

She needs to win. And not just for the money. For her, winning has never been about money.

Dusty's new teacher invites Elle and Roland to a parent-teacher conference. Roland takes the morning off, and he and Elle drive to the school together.

Dusty's teacher, Miss Sink, is younger than most of the waitresses where Elle works, with cleavage showing between the lapels of her dress. Roland looks her up and down. Elle knows what he's thinking. *I used to be a musician. There was a time when you would've stood in line to fuck me.*

"Dusty's speech has improved dramatically," Miss Sink says, her own enunciation so precise she sounds like she's chewing the words. "He's doing well in all his subjects. But we're having a little problem with his conduct. He passes notes in class." She hands Elle a page from Dusty's memo pad. On it is a drawing of a skunk, very lifelike, except the skunk has Miss Sink's face—her wide eyes, her clotted eyelashes, her snub nose, her pursed mouth. Under the picture is a caption: "Miss Stink."

Roland studies the picture. "This is good. Where'd he learn to draw like this?"

Miss Sink tugs at her dress as if it's suddenly too tight. "If this were Dusty's only drawing," she says, sniffing, "I wouldn't have called you in. But he constantly disrupts the class with his notes. I had to confiscate his pad."

"He needs his pad," Elle says, even though all she has to do is buy him another one. Fifty-nine cents. "It's like a body part."

"Then he needs to learn to use it responsibly."

"We'll talk to him," Roland says. He puts his hand on Elle's back.

"That's all I'm asking," Miss Sink says.

She escorts them to the classroom door and thanks them for coming. Elle pulls the door shut behind them, harder than she means to, hard enough to rattle the glass pane. She can't believe she just gave up a morning at her machine for this.

One evening when she is alone with Dusty, she asks him, "Would you like a little brother?"

He is sitting on the floor, drawing. He doesn't look up. "Not little," he says. "Big."

Of course, Elle thinks. A big brother could take care of him, teach him things. Rescue him from his parents. From a mother who tries too hard to love him, and a father who tries too hard to love his mother.

Elle has promised to take Roland and Dusty fishing. She buys them rods and reels. She packs a cooler with cheese sandwiches and navel oranges and water bottles. Dusty fills his CD notebook, Elle fills the car with gas, and the three of them head north on Highway 445, toward Pyramid Lake. The road is empty, the desert huge and pale.

"This is where my parents died," Elle says, more to herself than anyone else. "Somewhere out here." There is no white cross to mark the place where her parents' car burned.

"What's it like to die?" Dusty asks from the back seat.

Roland says over his shoulder, "You're too young to worry about dying, buddy. Let's listen to some tunes. What'd you bring?"

"When people die," Dusty says, "they leave and don't come back."

"Did you bring any Ry Cooder?"

"Honey," Elle says, "nobody knows what it's like to die." She watches Dusty in the rearview mirror. He is flipping through his CDs, his face blank, innocent.

When her parents died, her uncle told her their time had come. She wonders if that's true, if people carry their deaths inside them like flowers that know when to bloom.

"Death," Roland says in the loud, sure voice he uses when he doesn't know what he's talking about, "is like the desert." He points out the window. "Like this. A whole lot of nothing, forever."

———

Pyramid Lake belongs to the Paiute Indians.

According to legend, a man from the Paiute tribe traveled to the California coast where he fell in love with a "woman of the sea"—a mermaid, whom he was forbidden to marry. But he married her anyway, in secret, and took her home with him. They had clear weather for the first part of the journey, but when they crossed the mountains at Tahoe, it began to rain. Rain came down in torrents. It followed the couple through the Truckee meadows, all the way to what is now Pyramid Lake.

The mermaid could not bear children, so—the legend goes—she stole babies from the Paiute women and took them to live with her in the lake. You can hear them even now, the Indians say: high, gurgly sounds that can't be explained by the wind or any force of nature except the spirits of the stolen babies, crying for their mothers.

Elle's mother claimed she'd once heard the water babies. She was visiting a friend who lived by the lake, and one afternoon she and her friend heard small voices crying and water splashing. They followed the sounds to the lake and looked all around, but there was no one. In every direction, the lake—bright blue, a mirror of the sky—was empty. As soon as they realized what they must be hearing, they closed their eyes. "Bad things happen if you see them," Elle's mother said.

Elle and Dusty and Roland fish from the dock at Pelican Beach. Dusty drops his line into shallow water and catches a small suckerfish, which Elle makes him throw back. First, though, he stoops down and pets the fish. "Goodbye, sucker," he says. The words come out perfectly.

Elle and Roland look at each other and laugh. Elle can't remember when they last laughed at the same time for the same reason.

———————

In the summer there are wildfires in the desert. The sky rains ashes.

The heat in the grocery store parking lot is brutal, but inside, the store is an oasis—cool and clean as a hospital, with wide aisles and fluorescent lights and waxy green-and-white checkered floors. Elle lets Dusty push the cart. He reads the grocery list aloud and she picks items off the shelves. This is good practice for him. He can pronounce all the words, but he still has trouble controlling his volume and sometimes sounds like a broadcaster.

"PANCAKE MIX!" "APPLESAUCE!"

"That's good, honey," Elle says, ignoring the people who stare.

In the frozen food section, Dusty sneaks a box of ice cream sandwiches into the cart. Elle pretends not to notice. This is a game they play every week.

They find the shortest checkout line and Dusty arranges their groceries on the conveyor while Elle sorts her coupons. The cashier calls out the total, Elle writes a check, and the cashier feeds it into her computer. After a few seconds, a message appears on the screen. The cashier calls for her manager, a man so young he still has pimples.

"I'm sorry, ma'am," he says to Elle. "We'll need another form of payment."

Elle pulls out a card.

"Not an ATM card," he says. "Cash or credit."

Elle fishes through her purse. She takes out her credit card and tries swiping it. The card is declined.

"What would you like to do?" the manager asks. "Is there someone you can call?" His voice sounds like it might break if he's forced to keep talking.

Glorified bag boy, Elle thinks. "I'd like to talk to your supervisor," she says.

"I'm sorry, ma'am. I'm the only manager on duty. We can hold your items for a few minutes if you like."

People are lining up. The conveyor is already loaded with the next person's groceries.

Dusty is at the end of the counter, rattling through the bags in their cart. He digs out his box of ice cream sandwiches. "I'll put these back," he offers.

"It's okay, honey," Elle says. "It's not your fault. Put your ice cream down and let's go." She grabs his hand and marches him out of the store, leaving their groceries behind.

Outside, the air feels like fire. Ashes have coated the car.

Elle wasn't allowed to see her parents after they burned. She had to imagine their bodies. The image, stronger than a memory, still sickens and fascinates her. She wonders what her own death will look like. If it's taking shape in her even now.

She puts her key in the ignition, turns on the windshield wipers, pushes the washer button, and the ashes on the glass turn to mud.

III.

MISSING

Other Mothers' Sons

Addie is paying the cashier, not paying attention to her groceries, and the bagger hands them to a young boy who's loitering at the end of the checkout aisle. "He isn't mine," Addie says, though looking at the boy, she realizes he could be. Dark haired, dark eyed. He even dresses like Roland used to, in a collared shirt and corduroy pants. He's clumsy like Roland, too, and spills one of her bags when he sets it down.

"*Uh*-oh," Addie says in the singsong voice she uses with children.

The boy blushes and runs to his mother, in line behind Addie. Addie tries smiling at him, her most reassuring smile, but the boy doesn't smile back. He burrows under his mother's arm, hiding.

"Do you need a hand with these?" The bagger has repacked her spilled groceries.

"Thanks," Addie says, still smiling uselessly. "I think I can manage."

———

She can't help talking to them, all the boys who could be Byrd; she can't help wanting to know them. What do they like to read, what are their favorite subjects in school? Do they play sports? How old are they? When's their birthday? They give clipped, offhand answers. Sometimes their mothers are gracious and encourage them to talk. Some mothers tilt their heads, sorry for Addie. Some are nervous and possessive, moving closer to their sons, owning them.

Addie takes nothing personally. They're just acting on instinct, like her.

Dear Byrd,
Say I looked for you. Say I found you. What then? You belong to someone else.

The Internet lists a local group with an acronym that, if you saw it on a license plate, you would read as "trouble." Or "turble," the way some people say "terrible." You wouldn't think Triangle Region Birthparents Liaison. She calls the number, and a woman picks up on the first ring. Dotty Waters, her voice chirpy and hopeful.

Dotty's organization—"Tribble," she pronounces it, like something you'd wipe off a baby's chin—has had "phenomenal success" connecting parents with their children, "which as you know," Dotty says, "is not an easy thing to do in this backwards state. In North Carolina, two grown people who want to meet each other can't." Dotty started by finding her own daughter, then helped a friend find *her* child, then decided to open her own voluntary registry.

In the background Addie can hear a television. Every now and then Dotty stops talking to make clucking noises—at a dog or a cat maybe, or a caged bird.

"If you're ready," Dotty says, "we'll get you registered and start to work on your reunion. Let's start with your son's date of birth."

"The fourteenth of September, nineteen eighty-nine," Addie says. "But I'm not interested in a reunion. I just want to locate him." She uses that word, "locate," because it sounds unintrusive, like something one does from a safe distance.

"Oh, sweetie," Dotty says, deflating. "I'm so sorry. He's only ten. There's nothing we can do yet."

"I'm not trying to meet him. That's what I'm telling you. I just want to know where he is. I want to know he's okay."

"This is only a registry, sweetie. We don't do investigations."

"I need an investigator?"

"No. Not yet. There's nothing an investigator can do until your son turns eighteen. Which is not to say there aren't people out there willing to take your money. All those guys listed in the yellow pages? Retired cops. Oh, sure, they know a few tricks, but they don't know a thing about adoption. They'll be just as lost as you are." She clucks again and says sharply, "Down!"

Addie checks the yellow pages anyway, out of curiosity, and calls the first investigator listed. He admits that this particular kind of search is outside the scope of his experience, but says he'd like an opportunity to try.

"So how would you go about it?" Addie asks. "Specifically? I mean, you can't unseal the records."

"No, ma'am. I would generate a list of candidates using all available information. Then I would use investigative techniques developed over my career to narrow the list. I have a national network of retired law enforcement investigators. I have contacts in every state. If we need to look in Texas, for example, I have contacts."

"Texas."

"Just a for-instance. Of course, we'd start in-state. It's entirely possible your son is living close by."

"I've heard of that happening," Addie says. "Parents and children seeing each other without knowing it."

He has no idea how long the search will take. A retainer of two thousand dollars should be enough to get him started.

"I don't want to give false hope, ma'am," he says, "but it's entirely possible we'll get lucky."

"Thanks," Addie says. "But I don't have two thousand dollars' worth of luck."

Warren Finch is still in Greensboro, still living in his mother's house. Still wearing his big wristwatch, his plaid clothes.

"Your timing coming here today is very interesting," he tells Addie. He is holding a book the size of an unabridged dictionary, *The American Ephemeris of the Twentieth Century*. "Because of the transit of Uranus"—he pronounces it your-*ann*-us—"both you and the child are undergoing huge revolutions. For you, this is a time for expansiveness, for taking action, taking risks."

They are sitting in Warren's mother's rickety chairs, Warren with his giant book in his lap, fumbling through the pages. The house smells the way Addie remembers, like incense and cat litter, though she has never seen a cat.

"There's a karmic relationship between your chart and the child's, a reverse nodal situation. This suggests that early in the child's life you created a sense of unpredictability for him."

"Which we know," Addie says.

Warren glances up, his chair teetering slightly. "The child," he continues, "has entered a volatile emotional period in which he feels himself at the mercy of mysteries that date back to infancy. His family and surroundings feel insecure and un-predictable. And this is just the beginning. A longer-term life change is underway. There's a lot of conservative energy in his chart—he's a Virgo with three planets in Capricorn—so the part of him that wants safety and structure is feeling out of control. He could overreact, develop somatic problems because he's trying so hard to figure everything out during a period that calls for a different kind of response."

He closes his book, waits for her to talk.

She has nothing to say. She can't even look at Warren. She looks at the pictures of Buddha taped to his wall. Most of the Buddhas are seated in the lotus position, hands in their laps, fingers lightly touching. One is standing with both hands raised. He is laughing, but not serenely. He looks deranged.

"I'm sorry," Warren says. "Would you like a cup of tea? I forgot to offer."

Does he do this on purpose? Addie wonders. Upset her just to have the chance to comfort her?

"I'm fine," she says, and tears a check out of her checkbook.

How long do African violets live? Is it possible the blue one in Janet's window is the same one as before, that she's kept it alive this long? The picture of Janet's children is different, though the children haven't changed much—older but still plain-looking, in a plain wooden frame.

"I was hoping you could give me an update," Addie says. "I was hoping maybe you'd gotten another letter."

"I'm sorry," Janet says. "I haven't. The parents don't have to send updates, and I can't ask. I can't contact them at all unless"—she gives Addie a meaningful look—"I have updated medical history for *them*. That kind of information can some-times generate a response."

"Updated medical history like my father died?"

"Yes," Janet says, and makes a note in the file. "I'm so sorry. When?"

"In 1994, of a heart attack. You can tell them that."

The Readery has moved from the old neighborhood to a strip mall on Holden Road. The new store is big and square and bright, with plate-glass windows and fluorescent lights and wall-to-wall carpet and a three-person staff. A smell not of books but of carpet deodorizer. No peeling wallpaper, no dusky yellow lamplight, no late-night hours, no professors camped in battered armchairs, arguing.

"I had to sell the house," John Dunn says. "Business exigencies."

He and Addie are in his office drinking Starbucks coffee. His walls are bare, his desk is metal. His padded chair swivels and rocks. He is different, too. His beard is gone, and his big glasses; his eyes look weak and tired. He's wearing an ordinary blue button-down oxford shirt. Addie has to remind herself he is the same man he always was, her old boss, her old landlord, her friend who took her to the hospital and stayed with her and gave her gifts and made her laugh.

Now he's telling her about his divorce, how his English-professor wife moved to England with another woman. "She looks like me," he says about the other woman. "I guess that should make me feel better."

"With or without the beard?"

It's late when she gets back to Raleigh. William brings over burritos from their favorite takeout. Also a ripe avocado, which he peels, slices, and arranges on a small plate. He drizzles on lime juice. He is always feeding her.

"I'm not hungry," she says.

He sits down and unwraps his burrito. "When are you going to tell me?" he says.

"Tell you what?"

"Whatever it is you aren't telling me."

His eyes are the saddest brown. She wonders if she will ever deserve him. "I don't know," she says.

The next day she makes an appointment with a lawyer, a young woman reputed to be the most aggressive family lawyer in Raleigh. Thanks to a cancellation, the lawyer has an opening in her schedule that afternoon.

The lawyer has short sleek hair and a sleek suit, red with black piping on the lapel. Her office is a gallery of diplomas and awards, all expensively matted and framed. As Addie talks, the lawyer narrows her eyes as if to demonstrate that she is listening intensely. It's this intensity, Addie supposes, that justifies the lawyer's hourly rate.

"Is there anything I can do?" Addie asks after laying out her predicament.

"To find your son? No," the lawyer says. "Not yet, and you shouldn't waste another minute thinking about it. But you have to tell the father. You have to tell him *now*."

comfort sweet

"I almost didn't come," Addie says.

"I didn't want to," Shelia says. "It was Danny's idea. These people don't bother him. Nobody bothers Danny."

"My store manager, Peale, says you should always go to class reunions because nobody can ever know you as well as the people you grew up with."

"That's because nobody changes," Shelia says. "Look around. Look at Danny."

Danny is across the room by the door to the patio, his glasses reflecting the lights. He's laughing, shaking hands, slapping backs, saying loudly, "Far out, far out."

"It's pot," Shelia says. "Pot keeps him in a good mood. We've been married twenty-three years. We've lived in four houses and raised two daughters. I've had two surgeries to fix my eyes. And the whole time, Danny's been stoned and in a good mood."

———

Dear Roland,

I went to Carswell for our reunion thinking you might show up, all the way from Nevada. Traveled the Farthest to Attend. What took you to Reno? The class directory listed your wife's name and your son's; it listed your job as "entertainment." I hope that means music.

The party was at Comfort Suites ("comfort sweet") in the ballroom. There were balloons and strings of white lights and a blue-and-orange banner welcoming the Class of '74. There was a long table with hot hors d'oeuvres. The whole room smelled like Sterno.

I wore black silk pants and a lacy blouse. I got a few compliments. When people compliment you now, they don't say you look good, they say you look good for your age.

It was BYOB and I hadn't brought a bottle, so I drank cranberry juice and soda all night because setups were free. Nobody but the bartender and Shelia knew the difference. Nobody ever does. People who are getting drunk always assume you are, too.

Shelia showed me pictures of her girls. She and Danny have twins, Mavis and Alice. I love the names—imperfect rhyme for non-identical twins.

I showed Shelia pictures of my store.

"I'd be a terrible parent," Addie tells Shelia. "I worry too much."

"I'll tell you a secret," Shelia says. "We're all terrible parents."

I don't know who started the rumor, but people were saying you were coming, you were there. I kept looking around for you, wondering if I would recognize you. Have you changed much? I imagined you showing up late. You'd

*have just gotten into town; you'd be starving. You would
ask me to come with you to the buffet. A Comfort Sweet lady
in a brown uniform would be refilling the artichoke dip,
stirring white sludge into white sludge. You'd say, too loud,
"Are we supposed to make a meal on this stuff?" We would
heap our plates with cheese cubes and meatballs and find a
place to sit. We would try to talk but the music would drown
us out. You would eat all the meatballs. You'd feed me cheese
cubes on a toothpick. Finally the DJ would take a break and
the blare would die down and I would work up the nerve to
tell you what I'd come to the reunion to tell you, what I'm
writing now to tell you. You'd stop eating. Your face would go
blank. I wouldn't know what you were thinking.*

*The music would start up again, a slow song. We would
dance to keep from talking. And people would see us dancing and say to each other, "Roland and Addie, at last," not
knowing we'd already had our at-last.*

But you didn't come. Why not?

*So there I was, full of my news and no one to tell it to.
Stranded with people like Little Bit, still so tiny I could
pick her up. Even in stacked heels she could barely reach
the bar to check her tiny pint of rum. She asked me all
the usual questions (did she have a checklist in her tiny
purse?)—marriage, family, why hadn't I come back for the
last reunion or the one before that? "J.C. and I would never
miss one," she said, meaning J.C. Green, her husband, who
was on the dance floor shaking his ass and doing the arm
motions to "YMCA."*

Danny and Addie and Shelia all dance together to "Build
Me Up, Buttercup." "What I want to know," Danny says, "is
why this class can't hire a DJ who doesn't suck."

———

Remember Roy, our class president? Roy G. Bivens, like the spectrum? After he got good and drunk, he borrowed the DJ's microphone and gave a speech. Good old Roy, so goofy and proud. "Aren't we a good-looking bunch?" he said, though surely our class hasn't lived up to his expectations. No doctors or politicians or astronauts or actors. One athlete, but he died. One lawyer, but he was disbarred. We're a class of booksellers, set-builders, medical assistants, mechanics, mill workers, heating and air conditioning crackasses. We have an average of two point five children. Half of us either stayed in Carswell or moved back after college. Most who left didn't go far.

Still, when Roy smiles his class-president smile and says he's glad we came, we can't help but feel okay. Special, even, for having bothered to get dressed up and come out to see each other.

There's something I need to tell you. I should have told you a long time ago. I'd hoped to tell you in person at the reunion.

The child, your child, the one you thought I wasn't going to have? I had him. Ten years ago in September. I don't know where he is now, but I'm told he's with good parents. Better, I'm sure, than we could have been. I've thought of looking for him, but everyone says it's too soon. I have never been known for my timing.

Sorry for the long letter. Call me and I'll tell you everything.

Love, Addie

At midnight the DJ summons everyone to the dance floor, and people line up and put their hands on each other's backs to form a love train, love train. Addie stands behind Shelia and latches on and they go chugging around the room. And maybe it's the song, or all the cranberry fizzes, or sheer relief at having made it through the reunion without having to confront Roland, but Addie doesn't want to let go. She doesn't want the train to stop moving.

Claree, Knitting

Claree knits to keep her fingers limber. On the backs of her hands are thousands of tiny creases; she doesn't know when they happened. The hands of an old woman. At least she doesn't have liver spots like some of her friends.

Her friends are all grandmothers now. They're always telling stories about their grandchildren, at church, at Biscuit King, in the grocery store. They act like the only reason to have children is to have grandchildren. They open their pocketbooks and take out pictures. Claree smiles and pretends to be happy for them. They mean no harm.

Sam's Margaret isn't able to have children. Neither is Addie, but for different reasons: no husband, and now, she says, too old. "Some single women adopt," Claree has pointed out more than once.

Knit four, yarn over, purl two.

She has always been careful with her hands, putting on lotion after washing dishes, keeping her nails trimmed and filed in perfect crescents, keeping the cuticles pushed back. If you're careful with things they're supposed to last longer. But she is only sixty-two and her hands hurt, so much sometimes that she's afraid to use them, afraid of the mess she'll make. She rubs ointment on them—a friend told her about a brand that doesn't smell like Bengay. She massages them. Wears gloves to bed at night. During the day, she knits.

Slip two, yarn over, knit two together, purl one.

No grandchildren. How can she not in her deepest-down heart take that as a judgment?

She is working with a fluffy pink yarn Addie sent, starting a complicated lace pattern. Addie says the yarn was made by a woman in Chatham County who raises her own sheep. Always the romantic, Addie.

Sometimes Claree thinks about the child she lost. This was four years after Sam. She and Bryce hadn't planned another child and couldn't afford one, so at the time she'd told herself it was just as well. A girl, she was sure, another daughter. One who would have grown up to be clever and good like her other children, but quieter, more content, more like Claree. One who would have stayed close to home, married a local boy, had a child. A grandson for Bryce.

What does the Bible say? Thou shalt not feel sorry for thyself.

Repeat row five.

Even though thou must live the rest of thy days alone.

When Bryce died, she thought at first she should keep the house exactly as it had been, his chair and ottoman in the middle of the living room, the TV under the picture window. Then she realized it didn't matter—no one was around to notice if she changed things. The TV went first. She moved it to the den, then got rid of it altogether. Now she listens to the radio. She keeps it tuned to WCSL. The announcers can be irritating but they're company. She likes the call-in shows best, *Talk of the Town, The Birthday Club*. She always calls in for Addie and Sam on their birthdays, to hear their names on the air. Last year Addie's name was picked in the drawing, a steak dinner for two at John Wayne's. But Addie was on one of her vegetarian diets, so she told Claree, "You use the coupon. Take a friend."

When Claree was first learning to live alone, Addie used to come home almost every weekend. Then she bought her store and moved to Raleigh. Now it's four, maybe five times a year. She sends mail instead: cards, recipes, newspaper clippings, books of course. She sends yarn and patterns for scarves she hopes Claree will knit for her. She calls. She calls a lot, checking up on Claree, usually with an edge in her voice like she's in a hurry.

If Claree should ever really need her, if something should happen, if a fire broke out, if—God forbid—Claree should fall, it would take Addie two hours to get here. A local daughter could rush right over. A local son-in-law could fix the things around her house that keep breaking. Unstick her windows and doors. Replace light bulbs when her hands are stiff.

This weekend Addie is in town for her class reunion, but she isn't staying with Claree. She's rented a room at Comfort Suites, where they're holding the reunion. It'll be a late night, Addie says, and she doesn't want to wake Claree when she comes in, or keep her up waiting. Claree appreciates the thought. Of course she'll leave the front porch light on anyway, just in case.

Knit one, purl three.

Claree would let a grandchild do all the things she never let her children do. Jump on the bed. Stay up late. Make messes. "You're a mess," she would say, and gather the child in her arms, and her hands wouldn't hurt, or if they did it wouldn't matter. "A little old mess."

Rich, Part One

The first time Elle went fishing with her parents, her father caught a long golden spotted fish with a red gash under its jaw. A cutthroat trout. He pulled out the hook and showed the fish to Elle, his hand pink with watery blood. "Look at its eye," he said. "See? A fish doesn't feel." And threw it back into the lake.

Elle remembers the eye, that flat look, the trout's fear that it was already dead.

She's been pawning things—jewelry, her mother's silver, things she thinks no one will miss. The last thing was Roland's guitar, the one he'd had since high school, an old Strat he hadn't taken out of the closet since their last move. She's been borrowing money from her aunt and uncle. They never ask questions. This is their way of being kind.

She wishes they would ask questions.

If they asked, she would tell them the truth. *I'm losing*, she would say. *I've been losing for a long time*. She practices in her mirror, silently, watching her mouth form the words.

———————

The only way to change her luck is to quit playing. She decides this will be her last morning at her machine. She's only come to say goodbye.

She has to wait. There's another woman in her seat, a tall woman with white hair and regal posture. The woman is perfectly calm, even when she hits a four of a kind. She plays the way Elle never learned to—as if she's used to winning.

The Reno post office is a big stone building, cool as a tomb. For Elle, picking up the mail is more than a routine errand. She's intercepting evidence: late notices, collection letters. Today, two yellow envelopes with glaring red past-due stamps. Also a pale blue envelope addressed to Roland. The return address—Raleigh, North Carolina—is unfamiliar. The handwriting is a woman's. Small, delicate, controlled.

She puts the letter in her purse to read later. For now, she has more important business. She is going to see her aunt and uncle. She's going to tell them the trouble she's in. They won't be happy but they will forgive her; they're forgiving people. They won't let anything happen to Dusty.

It's a hot day. She's sweating all over, even her hands and feet. She rolls down her car window. Is this what it means to be brave, to do the thing you're most afraid of? Reveal the thing you're most ashamed of? She feels dizzy, buoyant, the way you feel when you're in the deep end of the pool and you've just touched bottom and you're starting to come up for air. You can see the surface, the light above the water.

When she arrives at her aunt and uncle's house there's no car in the drive, no answer at the door, no note on the kitchen table. Is she supposed to know where they are? Did they tell her; did she forget?

She drives home in a daze. Her house, she knows, will be empty—Dusty is at school, Roland at work. She turns into the driveway, presses the remote for the garage door, and pulls in.

The garage has always made her feel rich—the metal door that closes behind her, the automatic overhead light. She parks and sits for a minute, savoring these little luxuries. The car is idling, the window still rolled down. The blue envelope is sticking out of her purse. She opens it and reads the signature first.

Love, Addie.

Roland's North Carolina girlfriend. The woman she had to move out for. It was New Year's, the year before Dusty was born. They were living in Venice Beach. She had to move in such a hurry she forgot things—record albums, liquor, her favorite blouse.

Remembering that time makes her head ache. She is suddenly tired. The heat in the garage is suffocating.

The letter looks intimate, two pages filled to the margins with tiny blue script. She can't read it word for word—the words are too small and crowded and she is too hot and tired. Something about a class reunion. *But you didn't come.*

Roland never mentioned a reunion. Did he know about it?

Pet would have told him, surely. She would have offered him plane fare home. Anything to get him back.

The garage light blinks off; the garage goes dark. Elle puts the letter down, leans her head against the back of her seat and takes a deep breath. There's almost no air in the air, only heat. She's drowning in heat.

But you didn't come. Why?

Roland didn't go. He stayed home with her. He chose her.

Her car is still idling; she's forgotten to turn it off. Her window is open. The blue letter is in her lap. She has that feeling again, of being under water, coming up. She's near the surface. There's light above. If she closes her eyes, she can see it.

Statute of Limitations

Addie had been certain he would call the minute he got her letter, or the next day, or the next.

It's been a month now, and still no word.

She can't sleep. At night she paces. During the day she is curt with customers. She argues with Peale, badgers the mailman. She fires Vivian—twice—and rehires her.

Everyone is afraid of her. Everyone avoids her.

Sometimes when she is alone in the store, she throws books—cheap paperbacks. Sometimes she screams. The screaming, finally, is what scares her into calling the lawyer again.

"What's he thinking?" she says. "What can he do?"

"You understand I bill for phone consultations at my regular hourly rate," the lawyer says.

"Of course." She is on the edge of screaming again.

"So let's start with, what do you *want* him to do? What do you want from him?"

"Nothing. Just to talk—I want him to call me. Talk to me."

"But *legally*, what do you want? I'm a lawyer; what advice do you want from me?"

"Here's what I want. I want him not to do anything that could hurt our son. I read about a case where a birth parent was able to undo an adoption."

"You're thinking of the Clausen case from Michigan. It made all the papers. Different jurisdiction, and a completely different situation. That child was much younger; her adoptive parents basically kidnapped her. Your son—Burt?—is ten. His adoptive parents came by their rights legitimately. They're the only family your son has ever known. Unless they've been bad parents, no sane judge would uproot the child now, even if the father did challenge the adoption. Which in my opinion is extremely unlikely."

"It is?"

"Yes. Any lawyer is going to tell him the same thing I'm telling you. He can't win. He'd just be throwing away money—a lot of money—and possibly disrupting the life of his child."

Addie pictures the lawyer in her red power suit, her wall of diplomas and plaques—was there a trophy on her credenza? But no family pictures anywhere. A family lawyer with no family.

"What about me?" Addie asks her. "Can he do anything to me?"

"You mean sue you?" The lawyer laughs. Her laugh, like everything else about her, is quick and sharp. "Only if by not telling him earlier, you somehow damaged him. If he's like most men, you probably did more damage by telling him the truth."

"I didn't mean to."

"I know, I know." The lawyer softens. "Ms. Lockwood, there are a thousand possible reasons you haven't heard from your child's father, most of them innocent. Maybe he just doesn't know what to say. The important thing is, you did what you needed to. Did you send the letter certified?"

"I couldn't. That's not the kind of relationship we have."

"So you don't know for sure that he got it."

"No."

"Can you at least call him? Ask if he got your letter. Ask what he's thinking. Make notes."

"I'm worried," Addie says.

"I'm telling you: don't be."

"If he did want to sue me, how long would he have?"

"Three years. Three years from when he first learned about the child."

"Three years is a long time."

"Not so long," the lawyer says. "You've waited a lot longer than that to tell him."

Words

Dusty's suit is too small. It makes him itch. His collar pinches his neck. In his right hand he's clutching a fistful of ashes, not soft ashes like from a cigarette, but gritty. They cut like sand. When his father nudges him, he holds up his hand and lets go and a gust of wind comes along and blows most of the ashes away. A few stick in the sweaty creases of his palm.

His mother. The last of her.

She had pale yellow hair and partly chewed-off pink finger-nail polish and a tiny blue ladybird tattoo on her neck. She fell asleep in her car. Now she is ashes in the desert.

He and his family are standing in a big scrubby field next to a road that has no traffic. He has been on this road before, when his parents took him fishing at the lake. The road where his mother's parents died. The sun is a giant white ball.

"Don't stare," his father says. "You'll go blind."

His mother had swimmy eyes. Sometimes she sang.

His grandmother from North Carolina pulls him aside. She is tall and old and thin and her nose looks like a beak. He has always been afraid of her. She squeezes his hand so hard he can feel his finger bones rubbing together. "I want you to remember something," she says, bending down so that her face is close to his. "What happened was not your fault."

Which is when it first occurs to him that it might have been.

He remembers the day his mother left their groceries in the store. How she marched him out to the parking lot, holding his hand as hard as his grandmother is holding it now, and talked to him in a low, scared voice. "Don't tell anyone," she said. "You hear me? Especially not your father."

He wonders if he was supposed to tell anyway. Sometimes grownups mean the opposite of what they say.

Things can happen so fucking fast. In an afternoon. You can come home from work and turn on the TV and fix your kid a snack because your wife hasn't made dinner yet. You go looking for her. She isn't in bed like she sometimes is. She isn't in the shower. She isn't in the yard. She isn't anywhere. It occurs to you—who knows why?—to check the garage. And that's where you find her, along with the mail, in the front seat of her car, which has run itself out of gas.

Dear Roland, you have another son and you owe money everywhere.

She didn't leave a note. Just the letter in her lap and the bills in her purse. Her face was tilted to one side. Her cheeks were red; she looked sunburned. His first thought was to lean in and touch her, but he was afraid of hurting her somehow. Even though she was already dead.

He kept Addie's letter to himself. No reason Elle's aunt and uncle should know about it.

———

Pet decides not to place an obituary in the local paper. This is one small thing she can do to protect her grandson. If anyone asks, she will say Dusty's mother died in a car accident.

She calls Roland every night and tries to talk him into moving back to Carswell. "A good place to raise Dusty," she tells him. "It would be good for you, too. You need your family."

"We're *with* family," Roland says. He and Dusty have moved in with Elle's aunt and uncle. People with, as far as Pet can tell, no background.

"At least get out of Reno," she insists. "Try someplace new."

"I'm tired of new places," Roland says. "Besides, Dusty likes it here, and I'm letting him call the shots."

"He's nine."

"Yeah, well. He can't fuck up any worse than I have."

"Roland. Language, please."

It's late. Roland is lying on the bed with his clothes on so that he can get up whenever he feels like checking on Dusty, two doors down. Dusty has stopped talking again. He sleeps curled up in a ball.

Across the hall, Elle's aunt and uncle are watching TV. This is how they spend their nights, propped in front of the tube with the sound turned up. Roland can hear thick, dull laughter from some late-night show.

He leans back on his pillow, arms crossed behind his head, and stares at the wallpaper. This is Elle's old room, her bed, her slippery chenille spread. He thinks maybe he will feel closer to close to her here.

"Write me a song," she used to ask him.

"I'm no good at rhymes," he would say.

"The words don't have to rhyme."

"I'm no good at *words*."

After a while she stopped asking.

Now he has words—rhymes, even—but no guitar and no money to unpawn it.

Little flowers on the wall
Dusty sleeping down the hall
In the night I heard him call
I never knew you at all

He imagines a backbeat. A low, breaking, Waylon-like voice. "*Country?*" Elle would say. She wouldn't believe it. Him, the bluesman, writing her a country song.

The words in Dusty's head are so loud he's afraid to say them, he's afraid his voice will explode. He writes in his memo pad instead: *I'm sorry.*

Some things they will never know about Elle:

As a child she was slow to talk. She learned by watching the Patty Duke show. She called her father Pop-o, like Patty, and said bah-ee for bye like Patty's British cousin.

As a teenager, after she'd moved in with her aunt and uncle, she often went exploring in neighbors' houses while the neighbors were at work. In those days, in that neighborhood, no one locked their doors. She never took anything, only looked—in closets and dresser drawers, under beds, in medicine cabinets, laundry hampers, kitchen pantries, refrigerators. It was a game, to figure people out by the contents of their houses. She learned more about those people than anyone would ever know about her.

Some things she never knew:

She was right about Roland. He'd chosen not to go to his reunion, though he sometimes missed Carswell, those people.

She was right about Pet offering to fly him back to North Carolina, and Dusty, and Elle, too, if she wanted to come.

"Too expensive," Roland had told his mother. "If you're going to spend that kind of money, give us cash. We're saving for a house."

Roland has not been able to call Addie. He's afraid of what he might say. Still, he can't keep ignoring her. They have a kid—how did *that* happen? And why did she wait so long to tell him?

Bigger question: After ten years, why fucking bother?

He's in the car, leaving work. He stops for gas and a six-pack. While the clerk is ringing him up, he pulls a postcard out of the rack by the register, a picture of the Reno arch. "Biggest Little City in the World." Twenty-five cents.

Driving home, he imagines what he'd like to write. *Dear Addie, my wife read your letter and killed herself, and now my son, the one I'm raising, the one I've known since he was born, doesn't have a mother. Thanks for getting in touch.*

Almost

On the day her store is robbed, Addie is away at an estate sale, buying a rare set of Sandburg Lincolns. She also picks up a grab-box for William. She doesn't open it. She wants to be surprised along with him.

She remembers the grab-box John Dunn gave her when she came home from the hospital without the baby. It had a set of shrimp forks, three crocheted doilies, a dead chrysanthemum, and—the treasure—a pair of worn-out bedroom slippers, an old woman's dirty terry-cloth mules, fastened together with a plastic thread, no doubt by the tagger at the sale, but John Dunn pretended the fastener was the original, that the old woman had never bothered separating her slippers. "It was the shoes that killed her," he said, and slid his big feet into them and imitated the old woman shuffling around her house, her tiny steps unable to keep up with the rest of her body. He pitched forward, flailed his hairy arms, and landed in a heap.

Addie laughed, a loud, raw, ragged, awful laugh.

She wouldn't laugh now. The older she gets, the less funny the thought of falling, especially falling alone.

Peale is evangelical about "spreading the words," as he calls it. He thinks of bookselling as a helping profession, like therapy or ministry or law or medicine or matchmaking. To be good at it, you have to know your customers.

His first customer this morning is Mr. Olivetti, a small, stooped man who never shops but simply asks Peale to pick something out, buys it, takes it home and reads it. He records the title in a small memo pad he carries in his shirt pocket like a birdwatcher's life list, then comes back in asking for new recommendations, never commenting on what he's just read. Some people just don't know how to talk about books, or think they don't, or that they're not supposed to. That doesn't mean they aren't changed by them. Today Peale sends Mr. Olivetti home with three Vonnegut novels that just came in, old paperbacks in excellent condition: *Slaughterhouse-Five*, *Breakfast of Champions*, and *Cat's Cradle*. Who better than Vonnegut to change an old man?

Next it's Bunny Miller with her weekly donation—a stack of historical novels and inspirational memoirs, all new titles, the books immaculate.

"Did you actually read these?" Peale asks her, as always. It's hard to believe she could go through so many books and not leave a trace of herself in any of them. A mark or a dog-eared page or a cookie crumb.

Bunny answers, as always, "Why else would I give them to you?"

She always takes payment in store credit, which she never redeems. She could donate her books to the library for a tax deduction; Peale has pointed this out. Apparently she prefers the role of private benefactress.

Peale holds up one of the memoirs from this morning's stack, a critically acclaimed bestseller. "What'd you think?"

"Hmp," she says. "It's okay. Nothing I couldn't have written myself."

"You *should* write a book, Mrs. M."

"What on earth would I write about?"

"Write about everything you've read since Mr. M died."

Bunny is a widow whose worst fear is having time on her hands and nothing to read. She purses her wrinkled old mouth, looks pensive. "Not a bad idea," she says. "I could call it *After Albert.* Alliterative titles do quite well, I've noticed."

As she wobbles out of the shop, a tattooed girl charges past her in a hurry, demanding "anything by Jane Austen." ("A Jane Austen emergency," Peale will say during his police interview.) Then a middle-aged mother comes in with her young son. The woman is looking for a book she read as a child, an autobiography, Gerald Durrell's *My Family and Other Animals.* Peale checks the shelf. "Sorry," he says. The woman's son has dark hair and dark eyes and wears a backwards baseball cap that mashes his ears out to the sides. He isn't one of those glazed-over video-game kids you see. He studies the shop as if it's a foreign country. When he handles books he's delicate, touching them with his fingertips. He slides a volume from the rare book shelf. *The Happy Hollisters.*

"That's a great series," Peale says, "if you like mysteries. Something happens on every page. I read them when I was your age, when everybody else was reading the Hardy Boys. How old are you? Nine, ten?"

The boy doesn't answer. He is already reading.

"How much for the set?" the mother asks.

Peale is surprised. She doesn't strike him as an impulse buyer or the kind of mother who routinely lavishes expensive gifts on her kid.

"It isn't the complete series," Peale says, "just the first ten. But it's pretty rare to find them in sequence like this." He tells her the price and she pays in cash: one hundred and sixty dollars, his biggest single sale of the month. "If you want to leave your phone number," he says, handing her the pencil from behind his ear, "I'll call you if we run across the Durrell."

At eleven thirty, Vivian tells Peale, "I'm taking my break."

Vivian is in a dark mood. Selling books was supposed to be a temporary job, a phase—part of her young, hip, underpaid, intellectual single life. Now she's thirty-two and doesn't even like to read anymore. Reading reminds her of everything she doesn't have and probably never will.

She uses her morning break to meditate. Even a few minutes of silent chanting can help. "May I be happy, may I be satisfied." She sits cross-legged on a small padded bench in the children's section. Once or twice she is interrupted by customers; each time she returns to her chant. "May I have everything I need and want."

She hears the bells on the front door when the robber enters, but she can't see him.

"May all beings have everything they need and want."

He is wearing a torn Hawaiian shirt over a turtleneck, khaki pants, scuffed boots. His gray hair is pulled back in a thin, greasy ponytail. He has a cell phone pouch clipped to his belt.

"Where's your Ayn Rand section?" he asks Peale.

"I wouldn't call it a section." Peale motions toward a shelf on the far wall.

The man walks to the shelf without stopping to browse. He pulls down *Atlas Shrugged* and *The Fountainhead* and carries them to the counter. While Peale is ringing them up, the man reaches for his pouch.

"Sorry, sir," Peale says, and points out the sign on the counter, "you can't use your cell phone in the store."

The man smiles. He has a capped tooth (a detail Peale will recall for the police). Without taking his eyes off Peale, he opens his pouch anyway and pulls out not a cell phone but a knife. With one arm, he sweeps the counter clean. The Ayn Rands, the store newsletters go flying. The scrap of paper with the Durrell woman's phone number flutters to the floor. Peale yells to Vivian and reaches for the alarm button, but the man is already behind the counter, flicking his knife across Peale's throat, a quick slice. He growls something Peale can't understand, shoves his hand into the open register, cleans out the cash and runs. The bell on the front door clatters in his wake. Peale, too angry to realize he's been hurt, chases the man, but the man is too fast. He disappears into traffic, leaving Peale in the middle of Hillsborough Street, bleeding furiously.

The emergency room doctor says the cut on Peale's throat is superficial. A nurse cleans it and tapes it with Steri-Strips while Vivian talks to a police officer.

"We're a stupid place to rob," Vivian says, trying to keep calm. She's glad she was able to get in a few minutes of meditation before the robbery. "We hardly ever have cash. Nothing we sell has any street value."

"Anyone else in the store at the time?" the officer asks. He is thirty-ish, attractive in a stiff-blue-cap way. He takes careful notes.

Vivian shakes her head.

"Crazy motherfucker," Peale says, rolling his eyes. His pupils are dilated. His reading glasses are on the tray beside his bed, spotted with blood. "I should have known."

"How?" Vivian says. She explains to the officer, "It's a used bookstore. Half our customers could pass for thieves."

"Ayn fucking Rand," Peale says.

When Addie shows up in the little curtained cubicle, Peale gets even more agitated. "I was selling!" he yells. "I was having my best day ever!" His eyes are wild. The wound on his throat looks like a zipper.

"I know, I know," Addie says, hushing him. She glares at the police officer and Vivian as if she can't decide which of them to blame. "Unbelievable," she says. "In broad daylight."

"Happens all the time, ma'am," the officer says. His face is pink. Vivian wonders if he is being chivalrous, trying to cover for her. Does he think she needs to be covered for?

"We have an alarm," Addie says. "We work in twos. What else can we do?"

"Have you considered installing a surveillance camera?"

"Like a convenience store," Peale says. "And we can start selling beef jerky and plastic roses." He narrows his eyes. "Crazy little Ayn Rand motherfucker."

That night with William, Addie is quiet. She is trying not to think about everything she almost lost, could still lose.

She gives him his grab-box. It has a trowel with a broken handle, garden gloves, broken binoculars, a half-empty bag of millet, a shoe horn, and two boxes of bobby pins. Nothing memorable like the terry-cloth slippers John Dunn modeled for her. But she will remember tonight anyway—William in her apartment, happily opening his box of stuff, thanking her, putting his arm around her, telling her not to worry, everything's fine, everyone's going to be fine.

Promising not to leave her.

Not leaving.

> *Dear Byrd,*
>
> *I grew up believing that nobody can take care of anybody. I was wrong. People take care of each other all the time. Just maybe not the people you expect, or in the way you expect.*

What Comes, Finally, Part One

Call him, the lawyer said. That was weeks ago. Addie said thank you and hung up, and paid the lawyer's bill when it came, and waited, certain that sooner or later, when he was ready, Roland would call her. *Always let the boy call you*, her mother used to say, advice Addie never followed until now.

She's still waiting. She has rehearsed their conversation in her mind a thousand times. Sometimes when she's alone she speaks the parts aloud.

I'm sorry, baby. The way Roland begins every conversation.

You? Sorry for what?

Sorry you've had to carry this secret around for so long.

That's my fault.

Do you know anything about him? Where he ended up?

No. I have a sense he's close by—not based on anything, just a feeling. Maybe we've even seen each other. It happens all the time, you know.

What does he look like? When he was born, I mean. Did he look like me?

Yeah, but smaller, and his hair was all wet and flat against his head. Not big and fluffy like yours.

They will laugh, the two of them finally in this together.

What comes, finally, is a postcard—the first piece of mail he has ever sent her. A glossy picture postcard of the neon arch over Reno, Nevada, "Biggest Little City in the World." On the back, in careful blue ballpoint, is her address with a blue ballpoint box around it, and to the left of it, this message:

> *Addie,*
> *I don't blame you.*
> *Roland*

That's all. In two months he has come up with a single four-word sentence. And Addie has no idea what it means.

I don't blame you for having my child even after you told me you weren't?

I don't blame you for not keeping him?

I don't blame you for not telling me?

She studies his handwriting for a clue, any sign of feeling. It's art, his handwriting. She has never known another man with such beautiful cursive. It hasn't changed since he signed her yearbook in 1974, or wrote on her Gladys Knight album cover in 1989. *Lots of love and luck, Roland Rhodes.* She has them still; she will keep them always—the yearbook, the album cover, now this cheap, shiny postcard.

They all mean the same thing.

Goodbye.

What Comes, Finally, Part Two

A week later, more mail—a letter this time. The envelope is from the Department of Social Services, but the letter inside is not from Janet. Addie recognizes the handwriting: neat, forward-slanted, school-teacherish. As before, there is no greeting. Byrd's mother doesn't know what to call her.

> *I'm sorry to hear about your father's passing.*
>
> *Our son, I am pleased to report, is healthy. No asthma. He even plays sports—baseball and soccer. He doesn't excel but he tries hard, which impresses me more than if he simply stuck to the things he's good at. Science and math and music.*
>
> *He knows he is adopted. This is still fresh news. We told him on his birthday. What a day, can you imagine? A bicycle with gears, a new baseball glove, some books, and oh, by the way, you're not who you thought you were.*
>
> *Ten seemed the right age. Of course the books all say that's much too late. They say you should start talking about*

it right away. But he's an unusual child. He has always liked structure—organizes his toys (to explain his system would take another, much longer letter), eats his meals off divider plates. We were afraid to unsettle him.

He looked at us like we were reading him a math problem. He asked the questions we were expecting: who were his real parents, why didn't they keep him.

We said what we'd planned. His parents loved him, we said, and wanted him to have a better life than they could give him.

Now he seems to be trying to figure out how he's supposed to feel. He has always believed there's a right way to do things, to think, to feel, and that if he pays attention, he can figure out what it is. Lately I've noticed him looking differently at women my age, women who are old enough. *He studies them in church, in the library, in the grocery store. If a friend's mother cheers him on at a ballgame, he turns his head and stares. He talks to the lady who feeds the ducks in the park. He seems to be testing for some spark of recognition.*

Do I need to mention that this is hard for me?

You must wonder if he will ever look for you. I can tell you: he's already looking.

IV.

GROWN

December 2007

Dear Byrd,

When my brother and I were young, we thought Christmas would be better if we had a fireplace, so our parents ordered one from Sears—bright red bricks printed on big sheets of cardboard, with a mantel sturdy enough to hold our stockings and a black cardboard fire with holes for an orange light to shine through. My brother did all the perforating and folding and assembling himself. Every night leading up to Christmas he'd say, "Let's turn on the fire," and we'd sit on the rug and imagine we were getting warm.

My brother liked figuring things out. On Christmas Eve he would lie in his room pretending to sleep, waiting for our parents to go to bed. As soon as they turned out the lights (all but the Christmas tree lights, which they left on for Santa) and closed their bedroom door, my brother would sneak into the living room to check for presents—not to open them; he just wanted to see them, to know they were there. He was proving his theory that in the very instant *our parents went to bed, Santa Claus would have come. For him, that was the magic of Christmas. Not the presents Santa brought, but the absolute infallibility of Santa's timing.*

Now our mother has an electric fireplace, a wall-mounted thing with synthetic logs and a heater and a fan. I don't know what happened to the Christmas fireplace.

I've spent every Christmas Eve in that house. This year will be no different. My husband is packing the car as I write. He's a good sport, my husband, and a methodical packer.

We married late—I was forty-four, too old for a big white dress and a grand entrance. I wore a blue sweater and a wool skirt and he wore his suit and we stood in front of a justice of the peace, a tall, stooped man with a cough, and read the vows we'd written. Simple vows. I will always love you. I will never leave.

I can guess what you're thinking: I'm not qualified to make such promises and don't deserve them. You're probably right. But there comes a time, even for someone like me, when there's nothing to do but throw yourself into whatever your life is. My life is a secondhand bookstore and a husband and a house on a hill and a pair of finches, green-wing singers who can turn their heads all the way around.

The man I married is not your father. Your father was a musician. Not famous, but he had a gift.

He married someone else soon after you were born, and they had a son, your half-brother. I never met your father's wife, though I once spoke with her on the phone—at least I think it was her. She died in a car accident years ago. By the time I found out, it was too late to send a sympathy card, even if I'd known where to send it.

I haven't seen your father since you were born. I've gone to two high school reunions hoping to. At the last one, our thirtieth, he wasn't even listed in the class directory. No one had heard from him. He's probably off somewhere leading a secluded and mysterious life. He never quite belonged to us, your father. He was never mine.

But you.

I looked for you, years ago. I've written you letters, a box full, all unsent.

This one I am mailing, because you're grown now. Your coming-of-age letter.

Maybe one day you'd like to meet me. Maybe not. I have hopes but no expectations. Here's one decision, at least, that gets to be yours. This letter is my invitation to you, a standing, arms-open-wide invitation to visit if and only if you want to, when and only when you're ready. I'm easy to find; the agency that placed you has all my information. I'm sure you have questions for me. I promise to answer if I can. Maybe you have things you'd like to say. I promise to listen. I'm a good listener; your father always said so. He once said that when I listened, it was like I let everything else fall away. If he ever loved me, it was for that.

Don't worry about calling first. Just come. That way if you change your mind at the last minute I'll be none the wiser. We have a nice guest room, freshly painted antique white (I don't know your favorite colors), with windows overlooking a creek. You can stay as long as you like.

For now, I should stop and post this so that my husband and I can leave for my mother's, a two-hour drive. When we get there my husband will insist on parking on the street, leaving the driveway open for people may or may not show up. ("Just in case," he'll say.) My mother's Christmas tree will be lighting up her picture window, a little tabletop tree with bubbling blue lights. We'll walk inside and the house will smell like ham and mulled cider and cigarettes. My mother will get up from her electric fire to greet us. She's probably camped there this very minute, toasting her hands, glancing at her watch, wondering if we'll be late as always. Wishing we were there already. Trying to be patient. Trying, as she does, as mothers do, simply to wait.

A Short History of Sam

He is a curious, careful child, touching things with his finger-tips to feel how they're put together, sometimes taking them apart and remaking them into new things with motors and wheels. He thinks, his whole family does, that he will become an inventor. No one thinks *claims adjuster*. No one ever does.

He grows up, marries, and at twenty-nine, moves to Bisbee, Arizona, because his wife wants to be near her parents and convinces him the desert air will cure his asthma. Which it does. But it doesn't erase the old panic, the sense that he could run out of breath at any minute.

Bisbee was once a mining town, then an almost-ghost town, then a town of squatters—artists, craftsmen, outlaws, misfits, refugees. Now ordinary people like Sam and Margaret live here. Bisbee is higher and hillier and usually at least ten degrees cooler than Tucson—where Margaret's parents live—and redder. Everything is red: red rocks, red hills, red as far as you can see. In a certain light it seems the whole world is on fire.

The days can be scorching, but the nights cool off fast, and the sky fills up with stars. Sam buys a telescope. He keeps a calendar of eclipses and meteor showers.

"Why?" Margaret asks.

He loves her but she is as incomprehensible to him as he is to her.

He takes a job managing claims for his father-in-law's insurance company. He does all his own fieldwork, driving around the state, interviewing people, taking pictures of damaged houses and cars. His photographs are his art: fascinated close-ups of blistered paint, scarred wood, crumpled metal, smashed glass. He builds a darkroom in the garage and makes black-and-white prints. He loves the closeness of the darkroom, its chemical smell.

Margaret complains that his photographs are taking over the house. She's tired of coming home and finding wet prints draped all over everything. No matter how meticulous he is, now matter how careful to protect the furniture, she complains. "I can't stand it. The mess, the smell."

Margaret wants to start a family. They have a lot of sex, more than Sam ever counted on. He knows he should enjoy this, and pretends to, but after a while it starts to feel like punishment.

The fertility doctor is Margaret's idea. Sam thinks the treatments are a waste of resources. All that money to make more babies when there are so many already. "Why not adopt?" he says. Margaret says, "Because you never know what you're getting." He wants to say, "When do you ever?" But he goes along. They cash in their savings and he learns to give the shots. He tries to do this as well as it can be done (he's like this about everything), with the least pain to Margaret. He tries to give the best shots ever given.

When the treatments don't work, Margaret blames him. She accuses him of not wanting a child enough. In fact, he has come around to thinking that having a child—his own—would be a good thing. Someone who might share his natural curiosity, his interests. Someone who might want to learn what he can teach. Someone to make him feel useful.

He misses North Carolina, even though he couldn't breathe there. He misses all the things that triggered his asthma—grass, shade trees, flowering bushes.

He misses his family. His mother can't travel but his sister visits from time to time. Her visits remind him what it's like to be with someone who loves him. He shows her around Bisbee, all the coffee shops and art galleries. He drives her to the desert and points out plants she doesn't know: saguaro, catclaw, ocotillo, jumping cholla. There are snakes and lizards and roadrunners on the highway. Everything is exotic and bright, suffused with light. "Like the bottom of the ocean," Addie says.

In the end, the surprise is not that Margaret leaves—he assumes when she moves to Tucson to take care of her mother that she isn't coming back. The surprise is that he stays. He has become a creature of the desert, his lungs accustomed to dry air, his eyes to long views.

He has been living alone for years when Addie shows up in the late spring of 2008. He is thrilled for company, if only to have someone to cook for. He takes out his vegetarian recipes—he has a folder assembled especially for Addie's visits. Breakfast pancakes with bourbon and vanilla and nutmeg.

Lentil loaf. Carrot soup. Spanakopita. He wishes she could stay long enough to try them all.

On her last night, he makes portobello burgers and a pitcher of his famous blue margaritas. It's a cool night, so quiet you can almost hear the moon lighting the sky. A waxing gibbous moon. They're wearing sweatshirts, sitting by the grill.

"I need to tell you something," Addie says. Her voice is hushed, serious.

"What's wrong?" he says. "Is it Claree?"

"Nothing's wrong. This is something I should have told you a long time ago. I'm telling you now because—well, just in case. I wanted you to hear it from me first." She sips her margarita, sets the glass down. "I have a child, Sam. *Had* him, and gave him up. He's grown now. He turned eighteen in September."

"A child?"

"Yeah."

"Born—"

"Right before you moved out here."

"But—" Sam has a strange urge to consult a calendar. He glances at his iridescent wristwatch—nine forty-four. Time means nothing.

A child.

There has to be a right thing to say. He wishes he could think of it.

He has no memory, not even a hint of a memory, of Addie expecting a child. How could she have gone through an entire pregnancy, had a baby and given him up without her family ever suspecting?

How could anyone be so alone for so long?

But he knows the answer to that question.

"Have you told Claree?"

"No. Not yet. Maybe not ever."

"A boy. A nephew."

"Yeah." She smiles, her face reflecting moonlight. "Congratulations. You're an uncle, Sam."

Making him sound important. Big and important as a country.

Rich, Part Two

What makes Addie feel rich is, of all things, the doorbell. Not one of those lit-up plastic buttons that chimes or buzzes when you press it; she and William have a real bell forged from steel, its clapper a small steel ball. A simple, beautiful thing, weighty and substantial, like the door itself, which is solid oak. First-time visitors don't always understand the pull for the bell. They hesitate, tug timidly at first, and the bell responds with a gentle tinkle that could just as easily be one of the wind chimes catching a ruffle of breeze, or a glass of iced tea clinking on a neighbor's porch. Addie is attuned to all these sounds. If there's a person at the door, the bell will ring a second time; the visitor will pull harder, too hard usually, making a bright metallic clang, loud as a window breaking.

This will set off the birds—two green-wing singing finches who live in a cage that occupies an entire wall of the dining room. They answer every sound with one of their own. Certain loud sounds—the bell when it's pulled too hard, sirens, the vacuum cleaner, the coffee grinder—can send them into a frenzied chorus. When Addie plays records (she still has a turntable; she and William can't part with their record collections), the birds sing along, trilling and turning their heads.

The doorbell was made by an elderly blacksmith in the Village of Yesteryear at the State Fair. Addie and William go every fall. They marvel at the bloated pumpkins and miraculously decorated cakes. They sit on bleachers in barns that smell of shit and sawdust and watch the measuring and judging of farm animals. They amble through the midway, whacking moles, pitching coins, every now and then winning some misshapen stuffed animal that they give away to a grateful stranger. They watch children on rides—wide-eyed, open-mouthed little ones spinning around and around in teacups, teenagers screaming as the Scrambler slings them and the Zipper flips them upside down.

On a clear day, Addie can sometimes coax William onto the Ferris wheel. She holds his hand. She loves his knobby, stained knuckles. She loves him for riding with her even though he's afraid of heights (a mural painter who spends his days on scaffolding!). She loves knowing that she will love him all her life.

It's a rich life. Richer than she thought possible.

Still, there's something, someone, missing. There's a hole in her that, on dark days, she worries she could cave into.

"Everybody has holes," William says.

"I'm the holeyest," she says. "I am the holey of holeys."

"Yes, you are," he says, and bows. His hair is thinning at the crown; she can see a tiny circle of bare scalp, pink and smooth. It makes her love him even more. If only that love were enough.

September 2010, a Saturday evening at the cusp of fall. The dogwood leaves are burning; the light is changing, the sun slanting at a sharper angle. The air is dry. Soggy summer is over.

Soon the nights will be crisp, the stars brilliant. Whatever is ripe will be harvested or lost.

Addie loves and dreads this time of year—the dying beauty of the trees, the way the world begins its slow surrender to winter. September is the anniversary of her own surrender.

Tonight she is home early, cooking dinner—a curry, William's favorite, with cauliflower and chickpeas. A giant stew, enough to feed them until they are sick of curry. The rice is in the cooker. She pours herself a glass of Riesling. The finches are quiet.

Outside, there is a faint tinkling. Wind chimes or doorbell? She isn't expecting company. She waits. The sound comes again—not tentative this time. A clean, clear slice of sound, announcing someone. The exact sound the old blacksmith must have heard in his mind's ear as he was working.

The finches flutter and chirp. *Who-can-it be be be?*

"Hold your tiny horses," she tells them.

As always when she hears the bell, she moves with deliberate calm. She sets down her wineglass, turns the curry to a low simmer, walks through the house to the front door—*I have hopes but no expectations*—and opens it.

Acknowledgments

Emma Patterson, you are my dream agent. Thanks for your belief, intelligence, enthusiasm, and friendship. Guy Intoci, I could not have made up a more perfect editor. Dan Wickett, Steven Gillis, Steven Seighman, and everyone at Dzanc Books, thanks for your vision and commitment. Caitlin Hamilton Summie, thanks for your grace in helping to usher this book into the world.

For their generous support, I thank the North Carolina Arts Council, Vermont Studio Center, the Weymouth Center for the Arts and Humanities, and—my home away from home—the Virginia Center for the Creative Arts, where much of this book was written.

Thanks to my mother, Martha Church, who taught me to love books, and to my late father, Max Church, from whom I inherited the habit of storytelling. Thanks to my brother and sister, Andy Church and Marty Hargrave; my sister-in-law and brother-in-law, Joni Walser and Wendell Hargrave; and my niece, Morgan Hargrave, for their unfailing love and help. To Marty, particular thanks for our discussions about childbirth. Thanks to my high school English teacher and champion, the late Mildred Ann Raper, who opened the world to me. Thanks to Laurel Goldman for pressing me to write this novel, and to the brilliant teachers who guided me: Patricia Henley, Angela Davis-Gardner, and Jill McCorkle.

Thanks to Joyce Allen, Paula Blackwell, Mia Bray, Nora Gaskin, Nell Joslin, Nancy Peacock, and Pat Walker, whose critiques were invaluable. Thanks also to Laura Herbst and Ruth Moose for inspiration and encouragement.

Thanks to my comrades Elizabeth Kuniholm, Henry Temple, Melissa Hill, Wade Smith, and Robert Zaytoun for making it possible for me to balance my writing practice with my law practice.

Thanks to Edith Votta of the Children's Home Society for educating me on adoption procedures in North Carolina; to David Baumann of Reno for introducing me to the legend of the water babies; to muralist Clark Hipolito; to astrologer Randy Wasserstrom; to my brother-in-law and fire expert Bob Rodriguez; and to Patti Huopana, formerly of Nice Price Books in Raleigh.

Thanks to the birth parents who trusted me with their stories: Megan K., Richard K., and Cathy P.

My friends have sustained me in ways large and small. To all of you, my affection and abiding thanks.

For extraordinary acts of kindness with respect to this book, thanks to Bill Verner, Elaine Neil Orr, Anna Jean Mayhew, Dr. Lucy Daniels, Alice E. Sink, and Tina Bromberg.

Last and most, my love and thanks to Anthony Ulinski. You are my reward for everything.